This book is a-must-read. The story line is good, the conversations between God and Peter have great humor, and the story is easy to relate with. It's an all around good book. It helped me to realize that what we may think are little choices can change the course of our lives, and that God and his angels are always watching over us.

—Thomas Hertzler age 14

This book portrays God as, not just the One who is ruler over everything, but who also has a sense of humor in the way He works in Eli's life. I enjoyed how the author shows a "day-to-day" basis of "Father" guiding Eli in the decisions he has to make. I also liked how easy it was for me to relate with, since it's about a teen and the things he struggles with during his years of youth. I think it's a book that every teenager should read.

—Bethany Hertzler Age 17

Eli is a heartwarming story that demonstrates the hope and joy we all can have in a relationship with our Creator through the sacrifice of His Son Jesus Christ. Even in the midst of life-changing circumstances, Eli still has hope in the knowledge of his calling and election as a child of Almighty God. The manner in which Goldsmith has woven conversations between

Father, Peter and "Thumbnail" throughout the story periodically gives the reader God's perspective of what He is doing to fulfill His plan through Eli and his bride.

—Fred Powers
Associate Pastor
Forgiven Church
Fort Worth TX 76133
forgivenchurch.tv

Eli

Eli

Greatness Begins

MICHAEL D. GOLDSMITH

WITH

MARILYN BIBZA CHILDRESS

TATE PUBLISHING
AND ENTERPRISES, LLC

Eli: Greatness Begins

Published by Tate Publishing & Enterprises, LLC
127 E. Trade Center Terrace | Mustang, Oklahoma 73064 USA
1.888.361.9473 | www.tatepublishing.com

Tate Publishing is committed to excellence in the publishing industry. The company reflects the philosophy established by the founders, based on Psalm 68:11,
"The Lord gave the word and great was the company of those who published it."

Cover design by Blake Brasor
Interior design by Nathan Harmony

Published in the United States of America

ISBN: 978-1-62024-401-2
1. Fiction / Christian / General
2. Fiction / Coming Of Age
12.06.14

Dedication

Eli: Greatness Begins was a labor of love. I would like to dedicate that labor to the best friend and greatest love a man can have on this earth. I would like to dedicate this to my late wife, Sharon Joyce Goldsmith. Babes, this one is for you.

—Michael D. Goldsmith

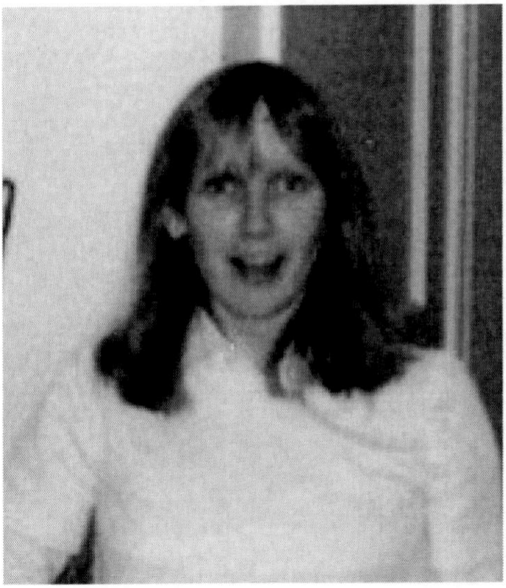

We serve a God of miracles. Through an absolute miracle, God brought Marilyn into my life to help me with this project. Being a retired Christian school literature teacher, she was able to help me avoid pitfalls that would have had an adverse effect on this project. Without her, this project would not have gone forward. She worked tirelessly on the structure of this project. She authored the educational questions at the back of Eli. Marilyn, I thank you from the bottom of my heart.

—Michael Duane Goldsmith

Table of Contents

In the Beginning, the Pain of It All

MPLS Gazette Tribune Sports, October 6, 2018

It was a classic showdown between Minnesota and Los Angeles in the Metrodome. No one could understand why we were in game seven of the World Series and Eli McBrien had not been seen since game one, when he struck out twenty-four batters in eight innings. Jon Thomas loaded the bases in the bottom of the ninth. There were no outs. Todd Rucket, grandson of the late Kirby Rucket, the great outfielder for Minnesota, was up to bat. He had a .400 batting average with thirty-six homeruns during the regular season. Against the LA pitching staff, he had been making all the pitchers look like rank amateurs. Henderson, LA's manager, walked out to the mound. Thomas was seen shaking his head. Eli had been warming up gently through the last inning. His arm seemed a bit sore. But when the game was on the line, they were going to go with their twenty-year-old sensation.

After the game, I asked Eli what went through his mind as he faced the hitter of hitters.

Eli replied, "I looked down from the mound and saw him standing there. Let me tell you, he looked real mean. So the first thing I did was ask Christ to touch his heart and draw Rucket to Himself. I then asked the Holy Spirit to guide the ball to where it needed to be."

Well, folks, this is what this reporter saw. Eli threw his first fastball at 109 miles an hour. Rucket fanned it. But then McBrien tried to catch him with his patented changeup. McBrien just about got caught himself. Rucket got a piece of it and drove it out of the ballpark. The ball must have gone 400 feet. There was one little problem. It was foul.

I could see McBrien give a big sigh of relief as he looked up to heaven. I could almost see his lips say, "Thank you." So now we had two strikes. McBrien knew what he had to throw. The problem was, so did Rucket. Both men knew it was going to be a fastball. They knew this ball would probably be the fastest, hardest ball that McBrien had ever thrown.

Now back to the beginning of the story.

Here was a time when a ten-year-old would see God's grace and caring through his pain and suffering. This would be with him for the rest of his life and bring him to greatness. Also, this was a time when Eli's heavenly Father would use people around Eli to touch him with His power and might in such a dynamic way that no one would be able to deny it. Finally, this was a moment when the true glory was not Eli's but God's.

Eli and his mom, Grace, were in the surgeon's office in Duluth, Minnesota. The doctor looked at Eli and told him what the surgery would entail.

"Can I see the x-rays?" Eli asked the doctor.

The doctor, with his warm smile, looked at Eli, put his hand on his right shoulder, and said, "Sure. Come into my inner office."

With that, they walked into his inner office.

"Eli, sit here," Doctor Thomas said as he pulled his chair out from his desk. "We don't do x-rays like we used to. Yours are right here on my computer."

"Cool!" Eli responded.

"Eli, your hips are not lined up the way they should be. When you push yourself, your hips throw your stride off. We need to realign your hips and spine. The pain from surgery is going to be like none you have ever felt before. Afterward, you will find that your running gets much easier and smoother. This will allow your pitching to be much more consistent."

Eli had only one thing to ask. "Will it make me be able to throw faster?"

The doctor smiled. "Can you throw fast now?"

Eli, with a tear in his eye, said, "Not as fast as I would like."

Dr. Thomas looked gently at the young man sitting in front of him. He said encouragingly, "Eli, you will be able to put more pressure on your hips once we get them aligned. That will give you the ability to increase the speed of the balls you throw."

Eli's mom had mixed feelings. She knew that in the long run, this would be the best thing for Eli. But she did not want him to go through the pain to get there.

The ride back home was not a quiet one as Eli about talked his mom's ear off. Eli was putting up a great act for his mom. He was going to be a man about this. He would not show his mom the pain he was going to be in.

It was about this time that his mom met a new friend. This friend had a close relationship with Jesus Christ. That friend's short influence would have a huge effect on the rest of Eli's life. This was going to be the first time anyone had ever laid hands on Eli and prayed for him. He would have his head anointed with oil, and the prayer would be one of power and confidence. The trust in Christ that Eli gained from this experience was something that would stay with him for the rest of his life.

This friend took Eli to his last game before the operation. Eli was able to get through the first inning having put a man on first. His outfield bailed him out, catching a fly ball and then getting the ball back to first for a double play. He needed only one more out. He was facing the other team's best hitter. Eli had been working with his mom in the backyard. He had almost gotten his changeup down. He looked to his catcher for the signal. He got it—fastball inside. *No way,* was the thought that went through his mind. *If this is the last game for me this year, I am going to try the changeup I have been working on with Mom.* Shaking his head, he signaled that was not what he was going to throw. The problem was that the catcher did not even know Eli had a changeup, no less did he have a signal for it. Eli smiled and winked at his catcher, Ryan Johnson.

What is he going to do? His catcher asked himself.

With a slight smile, Eli knew this was going to catch him totally off guard. Eli reared back like he was going to throw a fastball. The ball floated on him. The kid batting swung early, caught the ball, and hit a deep pop fly that was caught in the outfield. Eli breathed a sigh of relief because he was out; it could have been very bad.

When he came to the dugout, his coach pulled him aside. "Next time you are going to throw a changeup, make sure you set up your batter first," he said.

"How do I do that?" Eli asked.

His coach looked at him and gave him a little smile." You will need to throw him a couple of fastballs first, so he is timing them. Then you hit him with that changeup. It will totally mess him up."

Now Eli's team was at bat for the first time. Eli found himself batting ninth. The first three batters went down pretty quickly, and Eli was back on the mound sooner than he wanted to be.

Eli got himself into a bit of trouble, having loaded the bases. The friend, sitting with his mom, prayed that the peace that passes understanding and the gift of that peace would calm Eli and his pitches would be more constant. Eli settled down. He threw the first pitch.

"Strike," called the umpire. Then two more strikes were called.

Eli set up the next batter with two fastballs. Ryan, his catcher, knew what he was about to do. He gave a signal for a fastball low and inside. Eli shook his head. Ryan, in vain, tried to signal for Eli not to do it.

Eli had a little grin.

Tim, his coach, knew what was coming and smiled. He looked at his assistant and said, "Eli has this one set up."

Kyle, the assistant, looked puzzled.

Eli tossed the ball up and caught it with his right hand. He winked at the batter. He looked at the ball in his glove. Eli went into his stretch and threw what, to the batter, looked to be a fastball. Eli's arm came down fast, and the ball floated. The opposing batter swung half a second too early. The momentum of his swing completely spun him around to the left.

"Strike three!" the umpire shouted.

The smile on Eli's face could have lit up Shay Stadium.

Eli walked into the dugout. Tim gave Eli a high-five and said, "Good work." Eli grinned at his mom and her friend.

Grace looked at Eli and then at her friend and happily said, "He learns well. He really learns well. I am so impressed with my son." Her pride was showing through in a way that made even the birds sing with joy over her son. But soon, that joy would be turned into sadness over the pain Eli was to endure from the surgery and also over being taken away from the sport he loved.

On Monday of the following week, Eli and his mom packed the car and headed to Grace's brother's in Duluth, Minnesota. Grace could see the fear in Eli's eyes, even though he was putting up a very strong front. Her friend had gone home to run his business, so she was totally alone with no help with Eli. Grace and Eli drove toward

Duluth in silence. Everyone was nervous about what was about to happen to Eli. However, Eli had a feeling that this would be the key to his future success. He knew that in order to compete at all, he had to be able to run properly, and in order to do that, he had to get his hips and spine in alignment. The short pain would be worth it in the long run.

As they arrived at the hospital, everyone seemed cheery, but Eli could see the pain on his mother's face.

"Don't worry, Mom. Your friend prayed for me. I am gonna be okay."

Grace forced a smile back at Eli. She knew that Eli would hurt beyond his pain threshold. Her heart was breaking. But she knew that she had to trust God. After all, Eli was.

Grace's mind was racing. Some things had happened with her friend that put a strain on that relationship. Eli's dad was coming to the hospital. The divorce had been brutal on Grace. Eli's dad had left her with five children, a mortgage, and nothing else. He took all the money. Her courage in all this was what Eli drew his strength from. Because of this strength, Eli knew he was destined for greatness. He could see the vision in his mind. It was vague, but it was there. What was not clear, however, was whether his greatness would be in his guitar playing or in his baseball or both.

Eli had just started to play the guitar his father had given him for Christmas. Using a system that his mother's friend had developed, the friend was able to use a web cam to give Eli basic instruction on the guitar. Once Eli had the basics down, he was able to accomplish amazing things quickly and become quite proficient. Soon, Eli would be at the same level with his guitar that he was with his baseball skills.

While Eli and Grace were in the waiting room at the hospital, Eli turned white. His mom could see the fear start to well up on Eli's face. He looked up at her. Her kind eyes gazing back at him brought him comfort. Her soft voice soothed his spirit and brought him peace.

Eli's sleep the night before the operation was restless. He just could not seem to get comfortable. He tossed and turned all night. Feeling himself getting hungry, he buzzed the nurse. "Can a guy get something to eat around here?"

"I am sorry, Eli. It's after midnight. Our orders state that you can only have ice chips now."

For a ten-year-old boy with a high metabolism, this was a torture worse than death. He started to get very agitated. One could see his temper start to heat up. Eli started to pray. As he did, he calmed down.

The nurse came back into the room. "Here, take this."

"What is it?" Eli asked quickly.

"Just a sleeping pill. You will sleep with this. You need your rest," the sweet nurse said softly.

Eli took the pill. The next thing he knew, he was dreaming.

At 5:00 a.m., the night nurse walked in. "Eli, it's time to get ready."

Eli's eyes got big. He knew it was going to hurt. He realized the pain would be intense. But Eli remembered the friend praying for him. He knew his Lord, and relaxation came over him.

In the operating room, the doctor visited him before he is put under. "Are you ready to have your life improved?"

Eli just laid there. The doctor who was putting him to sleep told Eli to count backward from ten.

"Ten, nine, eight..." and Eli was out.

Upstairs, Grace was pacing the floor back and forth.

The nurse came in. "Grace, relax. Everything is going to be okay," the nurse said in a comforting tone.

Grace found a quiet place. She looked at the ceiling and asked Father to touch Eli. She also asked Him to guide the hands of the doctor. Grace's nerves were totally fried. She was concerned, scared, and worried all at once.

Grace looked at the clock. It was five minutes later than when she looked the last time. She found herself getting very, very scared. Then the thought went through her mind of her friend's prayer for Eli. She relaxed. Yes, she was able to trust God in this.

Again, Grace looked at the clock. She could hear it ticking. *Tick, tick, tick, tick,* minute after agonizing minute. *Tick tock. Tick tock.* One second, and then another, and then another. It seemed seemed like an eternity. She thought to herself to just get through `five minutes, and then another five minutes, and then an hour, and then two, and then three.

The nurse came into the waiting room. She said, "The doctor will be in shortly."

In a few minutes, Doctor Goldschmidt walked in and said "Eli did well. He is going to be fine. But count on this. He is going to be very sore for a while. He should be out of recovery in about an hour."

Eli's pain, when the nurse asked him to rate it on a scale of 1-10, rated at a 20. Eli moved around the bed, trying to get away from the pain that could not be escaped. But even in his inescapable pain, he could see the pain on his mother's face. These thoughts went through his mind: *I have to help my mom. I hurt, but I know she feels the way I hurt too.*

Grace was hurting inside. The pain her son felt, to her, was the height of a mother's agony. A mother will hurt seeing her son hurt. One can't help but imagine the feeling Mary had when Jesus Christ was on the cross. As she prayed, she felt a sense that she was not alone in the agony for her son. She knew that Mary felt the same hurt one hundred times or even ten thousand times more than she felt now.

The nurse walked in. "Eli, I want to give you a shot for the pain. Is that okay?"

"Yeah!" Eli answered enthusiastically.

The nurse gave Eli 50 milligrams of morphine. Eli very quickly fell fast asleep.

The nurse looked at Grace. "You better get some sleep too. Morning comes early here, and Eli will need Mom more than ever in the morning."

Back in her room, Grace prayed, "Father, please show me what I can do for Eli. I just don't know."

Grace tried to sleep. However, sleep did not come. She prayed again for sleep and got a nudge to call and get a sleeping pill for herself. The nurse gladly called the doctor and gave it to Grace, making sleep easier for her. Her phone rang at 6:00 a.m. She *reached* for her phone, still in the middle of a dream.

"Eli's awake. He is asking for you."

Grace crawled out of the warm bed and stumbled, trying to find the light. She felt the warm water of the shower splash over her. She felt the cobwebs starting to clear. Grace cut her shower short. This is one morning she would have really enjoyed a long shower. But she knew Eli needed her more than she needed the shower. Grace combed her hair and applied some makeup. Then she headed over to the hospital.

Walking into the room, she saw Eli in tears. He was in so much pain. She looked up to heaven and asked Father to take the pain. Just, *please, take the pain away.*

A tear was in God's eye. He knew Eli could take the pain He knew the pain that Eli was going through now was going to pay a high return later. Father, however, did hear the prayer about reducing the pain. If He had not, the agony for Eli would have been much worse.

One day quickly passed into another. Soon, the pain was starting to subside. Eli felt himself getting his strength back. The e-mails coming from Grace's friend every day have been a huge help to lift Eli's spirit and gave him smiles in the morning.

Finally, the day came. Eli got to go home. They brought a wheelchair into the room. Eli very gently is helped from the bed. He was still in a great deal of pain, but the pain was getting easier to deal with.

The nurse helped Eli ease into the Dodge van for the short ride to Grace's brother's house. Eli winced in pain as he slid into the backseat.

At Grace's brother's house, Eli was being treated like royalty. His cousin Tom asked to see his scars. When Eli showed them to him, Tom got a real puzzled look on his face and said, "They are so small!"

"But the pain is real big!" Eli answered.

Tom asked, "Man, are you going to be able to pitch next summer?"

"Doc says I can," Eli said as he ate his second helping of peanut butter cookie dough ice cream. A slight smile started to cross his lips as he thought to himself, *This is cool. This is my favorite ice cream. Everybody is treating me really great. I kind of like it*, he thought.

The next morning, Eli woke to the pain. He found himself crying.

Grace ran into the room. "Are you okay?" she asked.

"Just a little pain, Mom. I will be okay." Eli responded.

Grace knew this was true. He would be okay. But she hated the fact that Eli was going through all the pain. She touched Eli's shoulder and prayed, *Holy Spirit, please take his pain.* Immediately, she saw the tension leave Eli's face. Maybe, just maybe, it worked.

"Eli, how do you feel?"

"Mom, all of a sudden, it hurts a lot less," Eli said.

In heaven, Father looked at his angels and smiled. "Watch Eli. Just watch Eli. My Spirit has him. I am not going to let him go ever."

It was at that point, that Eli's life would be changed forever. He would know that God was real and, yes, He does have incredible power. It would permeate everything in Eli's life.

The trip back to Roseau, Minnesota, would prove to be a surprise, as Eli felt some pain but not nearly as much as right after the surgery. Eli found himself laughing and joking with his mom as they drove back. Pulling into the driveway, both Eli and Grace felt relieved to be home.

Eli knew that the rest of his life would be totally different because of what God had done for him and because of the people he had met.

The Gift Is Given

Anya pounded on Eli's bedroom door.

"Come on, Eli. This is the third time I have called you. Get your butt out of bed!" Anya yelled.

"Anya, go away. I just want to sleep," Eli responded.

"Mom says you gotta get up. Something about a strength workout with your coach today," his sister stated in a less-than-kind voice.

"Yeah, yeah, I know. The coach wants me lifting those weights to build chest muscles. It's supposed to help me get back to strength so I can throw a faster fastball. I am eleven. How fast does he think I can throw?" is the sarcastic response that a very sleepy Eli gave Anya.

Grace, who was walking by his room, looked in. "It's not how fast you can throw now; it is how fast will you throw in four or five years. Everything you do now builds for the future. Build it now. Get up!" she said, using her most intense mom voice.

What Eli did not know was that God was watching with His angels.

The Father said, "What Eli does not understand is that I am about to give him a gift that I give to very, very few people. If he is willing to work hard, I am going to give him victories that will astound people. I can tell when a person is young whether they are going to serve Me or not. Eli is going to serve me."

Christ, sitting at the right hand of God, looks at his Father, knowing what He had in mind, and smiled.

Eli crawled out of bed. The cold from his floor in the morning did not make for a pleasant experience.

"Why on a Saturday morning in January do I have to crawl out of bed to go work on the muscles for pitching when the season will not start until May, when school is out?" Eli asked.

St. Peter looked at God. "Does he always complain?"

Father chuckled as he responded. "He does, but that will change as he draws closer to me."

Bob Murphy, the school's weight coach, greeted Eli at the door. "Hey, young man, ready to get busy with a little weight training? This morning, we are going to work on the butterfly almost exclusively."

I hate that machine, Eli thought.

He went over, sat down, and started to work it. He had built up the weight from ten pounds up to fifty pounds.

He added another ten pounds today. As he worked the weights, the pain was evident in his face. But he worked it anyway. Grace was standing beside the coach this Saturday morning since none of Eli's buddies were there to see his mom watching him.

"Grace," the coach observed, "Eli has tremendous drive. I have never seen an eleven-year-old drive himself like this."

St. Peter looked at God. "Wow! What are you creating here?"

God smiled and said, "I am creating a super pitcher who will always give all the credit to Me. He will be able to throw a changeup that looks like the ball is streaking yet it is not. His fastball will be almost limitless in its speed. I see one problem. He is going to have the young ladies crawling all over him. As long as he keeps his eyes on Me, I can lead him to the one I have created for him. Believe me. She will knock his socks off!"

Eli was really getting into his workout. He was pushing harder and faster than he had ever done before. Both his coach and Grace watched in awe as Eli pushed and pushed harder and harder.

Eli smiled, as he knew what was going on. He was being driven. But he was not pushing himself. It was like something inside was giving him more energy and endurance than he has never had in his life.

Peter looked at Father. "What are you doing here?"

With a wink, God responded, "Just thought I would grant him a little extra energy today. He will be sore in the morning, but the muscles I am going to develop are almost as strong as I put into Adam back at creation. No one will ever throw as fast as he can, ever. I will see to that, and I will get the credit for this one."

Eli was sweating profusely. His mom looked at him and said, "Hit the shower, Bud. You will stink up my car."

"Be right back, Mom. I feel great!" Then he stopped and said, "Wait a minute. Why don't I run home?"

Peter asked, "Father, what have you done here?"

"Look, Pete," Father replied, "I just thought giving a boy a taste of what a runner's high feels like. I knew it would be a good experience for him."

"But, Father," Pete complained, "he's only eleven."

"You watch and see what I do with my super pitcher over the years. Just watch!" Father said.

"Eli!" Grace yelled. "Hit the showers! Grandma and Grandpa have invited us all over for dinner."

"But I could run over to their house," Eli responded.

"Eli, I don't know what has gotten into you. This new drive has me baffled," Grace stated.

Pete, chuckling, said, "Father, this is going to be fun!"

"My Word states that the body is the dwelling place of the Holy Spirit. Believe me. When I get done with this kid, it will be a great dwelling place! Let me tell you this, Pete. The young kids are going to flock to Eli. Many people will come to know Me through his life. But there is one person who has chosen not to."

Eli headed for the shower and told his mom, "Okay, Mom.

Grace looked at the coach. "What has gotten into him?"

The coach replied, "You know what? He is succeeding at something. Let him go with it. He has had frustration all of his life. He had wanted to succeed but has just had it out of his grasp. From reading to wrestling, success has just been out of his reach."

Peter looked at Father. "Is there anything we can do in this situation?"

"We? You are asking if there is anything *we* can do? There is something I can do. Remember, before I can do what I am going to do, he has to rely on My strength completely. I have given him strength that goes far beyond what he humanly possesses. When he puts his total reliance on Me, then you are going to see the superhuman feats of pitching. When his confidence is in Me, then things will become fun!" stated the great I AM with complete majesty.

Eli was sitting at the table with his grandpa, who said, "I hear you are working really hard there, Eli."

"Gramps, I can't explain it. It's like someone is inside of me. When I work out, I become like another person. I still don't like getting up early, but when I start, I almost can't quit," Eli said.

Eli's grandpa looked concerned. He took Grace aside. "I am worried about Eli and how hard he is driven."

"Dad, don't worry. I think everything is under control. Just don't worry," Grace said.

"You think everything is under control? I don't! That's my grandson, and I do not want him hurt!" Eli's grandpa stated emphatically.

"Dad, that's the same thing you said about me when I made the varsity basketball team my sophomore year. He's my son. Let me worry about him," Grace responded.

"I sure made a firecracker in her, did I not, Peter?"

"But how is her disrespecting her father going to help her, or Eli for that matter?" Peter asked.

"No, Peter. She was not disrespecting him. She was asserting her authority over her son. It is that attitude that Eli will need to get him through the toughest years ahead."

As Grace walked into the living room from the kitchen with Eli's grandpa, Eli looked at his mom and saw written all over her face that something was wrong. He knew from deep within what conversation just took place.

"Mom, it's okay. I love working this hard. My hips have not felt this good ever. It is fun being able to push this hard. It will be fine. Really, it will!"

Father watched the whole situation and said, "Pretty cool for my Spirit to reveal to Eli the conversation. I thought it would be a great way to keep everyone's mind at ease."

After a dinner of roast beef, mashed potatoes, corn, and peanut butter chocolate chip ice cream for dessert, Grace packed everyone in the minivan for the trip home.

The next evening, around 7:00 p.m., Eli was bouncing off the walls. "Can I call my coach, Mom? I need to start work on building my arm strength and my back strength."

"Whoa there young man. How have you been coming up with all this?"

"It is just there, Mom."

"Tell you what, Eli. We will look on the Internet and see what the professionals say are the muscles used in pitching. I just don't understand what it is that is going on here," Grace said.

"Pete, now do you understand what I have going on here? I have put it into Eli's mind what he has to do to succeed at what he is doing."

"Father, is it good for him to work so hard at this young age?" Peter said.

"Pete! Do I ever do things with people that are not good for them?" the Father's responsed.

Peter's face turned red with embarrassment. "I know you only do what is right and good. You always have and always will."

As she sat in front of her computer, Grace was typing into Google the following: "muscles used in pitching baseball." What she saw is exactly what Eli had told her he needed to work on. She looked up to heaven and asked, "God, what are you doing here?"

"I knew she would get it. Of course, I know everything, but I still get excited when one of my kids gets it!" God exclaims.

Grace said "Okay, Eli. Call your coach. You nailed what muscles you have to work on. You also have to start running to build your leg muscles."

"Mom, I am gonna throw the fastest fastball anyone has ever thrown or will ever throw!" Eli's intensity came through in a way that almost scared Grace.

"That's a tall order, but somehow, I believe you," she responded.

"Father, Grace has built a solid relationship with You. But how are You going to reach Eli?" Pete asked.

"Pete, the same way I really turned Grace on to Me. I am going to use her friend. You see, I have been using him for the last year teaching Eli guitar lessons. Only, I am going to have him start praying before each lesson. In one month, I am going to have the friend put a question to Eli. I already know what the answer is going to be. I have trained My servant well. He hears My voice. He is hardheaded at times and does not listen, making things tougher on himself. But I have and will continue to work on those areas so he can be perfected to be able to do all the things I have for him to do. You see, when I have someone ask a person to come to Me, it is at a point in his or her life that I know what the answer is going to be. I do things that change people's lives," Father said.

Grace reminded Eli, "Eli, remember your guitar lesson tonight. Our friend will be on the computer at eight sharp. He is taking the time, so we have to respect that."

"Gotcha, Mom. I always enjoy the lessons, and it's a great way for me to get to know him."

At 8:00 sharp, the phone rang. It was Eli and Grace's friend.

"Eli, how ya doin', man? Ready to play? I hear you have the new song down. I can't wait to hear it!"

"Wait till you hear this, Pete. Besides getting his pitching down, Eli is making real progress on the guitar."

Eli proceeded to play the song "Did You Feel the Mountains Tremble?" The intro was flawless. And he was really able to let the guitar do the talking with the rest of the music. The friend sat and smiled, knowing that God was going to use Eli in a mighty way.

"Okay. Let's do some jamming. We will work through this song a few times," Eli's friend said.

The music filled the house. One could almost feel the Holy Spirit as the music rang out the glory of God.

The guitar became a tool Eli could use in his pitching. As the music would go through his head, he could put pitches to music. For instance, he would be pitching to a top batter. At the same time, he might have Michael W. Smith's song "Secret Ambition" playing through his head, giving his pitching that much more power. He could almost hear and see the band he would start later. All of it would work together to help make Eli the pitcher God intended him to be.

Father said, "Peter, pretty nice touch, isn't it? Designing Eli to be not only a top-notch pitcher but also a musician! I will use the two to make both better. He will be on the mound, *hearing* my music as the ball goes faster and faster. I will have his changeup be able to slow down just before the plate. I am going to have fun because Eli will give me the credit."

Eli spent the rest of the winter at the gym, playing in his mind music while working out. Finding his concentration in school improving, one Saturday morning, Eli raised his weight on the butterfly machine by twenty pounds. It was the most weight he had ever worked with. Eli was an eleven-year-old lifting eighty-five pounds. At the speed he handled the fly machine, Eli had both his mom and his coach totally amazed.

Eli felt himself getting more powerful with each lift. His chest muscles were getting bigger and bigger. His back was growing stronger and stronger as he used the lower back machine to build himself up. All this was for a purpose that Eli (at this point in his life) had no idea of. It was not the purpose for Eli's life, nor even the purpose for him to play ball or learn the guitar. It was for God's purpose. Eli was yet to find out about that.

Eli worked faster and faster and faster. The weight went by ten pounds, and then twenty, and then thirty at a crack. He was even amazing himself. The coaching staff was getting very surprised at the strength Eli was building at a speed that they had never seen.

"Pete, this spring, I am going to have Eli throw an eighty-five-mile-an-hour fastball. I will guarantee that no one will hit it. Do you want to know the most important thing about this? I get all the credit," Father stated.

"Father, what if Eli does not give you the credit?" Pete responded.

"Oh, he will, Pete. He will," Father answered.

At home, Eli's oldest brother decided to try to bully Eli. He gave him a push.

Eli hit his brother Ryan in the mouth and put Ryan on the floor. Eli looked at his fist in amazement. "How did I do that?" Eli asked himself.

Eli saw the varsity baseball team practicing in the gym. He picked up a baseball and asked if he could pitch to one of them.

John Anderson, the best hitter on the team, winked at his teammates. "Sure, kid, pitch to me. I have not knocked one across the gym in a long time."

Eli found the spot on the gym floor that the pitchers had been using. He tossed the ball up and caught it. Eli smiled at Anderson and threw as hard as he could. The ball went in at eighty-five miles an hour. Anderson was not even close to it. A smile so wide you could drive a truck through it lit up Eli's face.

Father said, "Peter, now do you understand what I am doing? Here is an eleven-year-old kid throwing so fast that a senior in high school can't get close to his pitches. His pitches will be twenty-five miles an hour faster when he gets to his senior year. I will be exalted in what Eli is going to do both on and off the field."

"Father, does Eli have a choice in this?" Pete asked.

"Of course, Peter. He can follow me the rest of his life and see great things from both his music and baseball. If he chooses not to follow Me, he will lose both his music and his baseball skills." Father continued. "He will follow me. Just watch."

Eli was really turning up the heat on his workouts. His eyes were focused, and the look on his face had so much determination on it that it was almost scary.

Grace turned to his coach. "Should Eli be working this hard? He is only eleven."

The coach shook his head. "I don't know. I have never in all my years seen so much focused determination in a youngster like this. Never!"

"You see, Pete. I have everything under control. Eli is being set up to be the pitcher of pitchers. No one will be better, never ever!" The Great I AM said with a smile.

It is April. The varsity baseball season was in full swing. Eli was feeling confident in his ability. He had been throwing in the gym with an accuracy that would almost make the pros wince. Eli would have them tape a quarter to the gym wall. Walking to the other side of the gym, Eli would hit it with a fastball. Bob Johnson, the varsity coach, was looking at the rulebook to see if there was a way he could use Eli on the varsity team. The problem was, he was not even in junior high yet. To further embarrass the varsity pitchers, none of the varsity team could hit him. But they could all get hits from the varsity pitchers.

"Pete! Watch this! At the start of the varsity's first game, the coach is going to try to use Eli. The umpire will stop it when the other team complains. So I made sure the idea of a little demonstration is used. I put it into Coach Johnson's mind to ask for their best hitter just to give Eli a little experience."

"Eli! Take the mound!" Coach Johnson commanded.

Scott Nilson, the Bemidji Beavers' best hitter, came to the plate.

Eli went out to the mound, throwing the ball up and catching it. He looked at Nilson, smiled, and tossed the ball again.

"Come on, kid. Let's see what you got." Nilson yelled.

Eli smiled and looked at Nilson. He prayed for God to use this ball. Eli throws. Nilson fanned it.

"Kid, you got lucky on that one!" Nilson yelled.

Eli winked at him and threw a little harder. Nilson fanned it again.

Eli yells, "That's two, you oversized mule. You're not even gonna see this one!" Eli threw the ball as fast and hard as he could. Nilson stood there as the ball goes by.

"Strike!" yelled the umpire.

Yes, Eli got his first varsity strikeout, even though it would be three years before he got to pitch to a varsity hitter again.

Eli's Real Power

Eli had been working with the Lakeview Lions varsity baseball team, striking out batter after batter. He walked onto the mound for the first workout with his regular team. He looked down at his catcher, who signaled a fastball low and inside. Eli nodded in affirmation. He threw an eighty-mile-an-hour fastball and promptly knocked his catcher on his butt. Eli's coach's jaw dropped. Eli looked over at the coach, smiled, and got ready to throw again.

Coach Johnson walked over to the mound. "Eli, these guys have to be able to hit the opposing pitchers. In a game, then you can throw as fast as you want. In practice, they have to be able to hit it. Could you slow it down just a little, say, about half speed?" Coach Johnson said.

Father looked over at Peter. "Can you see what I have being set up? Eli's speed is beyond belief, even in middle school, and the coach has to slow him down in practice so his teammates can hit the ball," The Father said.

Eli's best friend, Hunter, was up to bat. His catcher, Terry, signaled for a low inside curve. Eli shook it off. Terry signaled for a fast ball low and inside. The coach knew what pitch Eli had in mind, and it was not a curve ball. Hunter saw the glint in Eli's eye and knew what was coming.

Eli thought to himself, *Hunter, you are not even going to see this.* Eli wound up and threw.

Hunter swung. The bat connected with the ball. It just about knocked the bat out of Hunter's hands. The ball was going, going, gone.

The coach knew it was a fluke but saw a chance to teach Eli a lesson about attitude. The coach walked out to the mound. "Eli, you and I know that there was something on the pitch when it hit the bat. The reverse velocity drove it. Eli, the other thing to keep in mind is this. You tried to strike your friend out. You tried to embarrass him by him not being able to hit you. I think God was trying to show you that if you get too prideful, he is going to let someone pound you. When you throw as hard as you do and take pride in yourself instead of what God is doing in you, then someone, in a fluke, will catch it. The ball will be out of there—not just gone, but out of there. Now go congratulate Hunter on a great hit."

Father said to Peter, "Hunter will not forget that hit as long as he lives. Neither will Eli," his coach stated in a fatherly tone.

Hunter grinned at Eli as he rounded third for home with his hands raised in triumphant jubilee.

The next batter to came up during batting practice was Samuel Johnson. Sam had gotten mad at Eli when he was playing on another team and Eli struck him out. Sam vowed to himself that Eli McBrien would never strike him out again. Eli knew that Samuel did not like him at all. Eli looked over at the coach. The coach gives him the signal to burn it.

Eli *thought* to himself, *Maybe I ought to let him hit it.*

The words of Coach Johnson come back to him. *When you throw batting practice, control the speed. Make them work for their hits, but their hitting has to get to the point where they can hit the other pitchers.*

Why then would Coach give me the burn-it signal? He looked over at the coach again.

The same signal was given: burn it. Eli shrugged. He looked down at Sam. He went into his set, threw about an eighty-mile-an-hour fastball. Sam fanned it. Eli looked over at the coach again. There is the signal again. Burn it.

Eli threw harder, at about eighty-five miles an hour. Sam swung again for strike two. Eli looked over at the coach again and is surprised by the signal, a changeup. Eli thought to himself, *Now I know what the coach was doing. He was showing me how to set up the changeup.*

Eli remembered how his mom had shown him how to bring his arm forward extremely fast, yet the ball slides off his fingers in such a way as to float the ball. Eli winked at Sam. Sam lost it and got really mad. The anger reddened his face.

Eli thought, *I've got him now.* Eli wound up and his hand came forward as fast as any fastball pitch would. But he did not snap his wrist the rest of the way. Rather, he sent the ball out like a shot put. The ball floated.

Sam swung so hard he spun around and he fell to the ground.

Peter looked at Father. "What was that about?"

"Pete, Sam cursed Eli. Nobody comes against my kids. So I decided to let Eli teach him a lesson. A very good one at that, I might add."

Eli asked his coach, "Why did you have me nail him?"

"Well, Eli, it's like this. When one of my ballplayers gets an attitude about another player, I always make sure it comes back to haunt him here rather than in a game."

As Sam walked up to Eli, he asked, "Eli, how'd you do it, man?"

Eli answered, "I have been lifting all winter. Mom and I looked up on the Internet what muscles I should be using and training. We started working on it. Look at the results."

Sam just couldn't figure out where this strength was coming from. He looked *at* Eli and said, "Let's go talk to the coach. I want to ask him a question."

"You boys want to ask me something?" Coach asked.

Sam looked over his left shoulder, not knowing that the coach was right behind them. "Where does Eli get those pitches?"

Smiling, the coach knew this was an opening that he must go through. "There is only one place where talent like this comes from: God himself."

"Pete, here is where it started. Eli just got the first words about my giving him his power his ability, his gift. Just watch as I keep building this building that I called Eli."

"Coach, I have never felt this much strength ever. I have not wanted to push this hard in the weight room ever. What should I do?" Eli asked.

"Eli, let's go for a walk." As they walked out of the gym, the coach put his big hand on Eli's shoulder. "I think God has something pretty special for you, young man. I know it has to do with baseball. I am not sure just how big this is going to be. I know it is going to be big. Eli, be ready to work harder than you have ever worked in your life. Be prepared for it not to end with this season or next season, but be willing to go for the long haul."

"Coach, I am only eleven years old. Would God use a young kid like me to do anything?" Eli asked.

"David was young when God anointed him as king. Samuel was only a lad when God anointed him to be a prophet. Joseph was young when God started him on his way to Egypt to save Israel from a famine. God is not afraid to use young people if they are willing to be used. God wants to use you, Eli!"

"How?" Eli asked.

"The concept, at this point in your baseball career, might be a bit much for you to handle. But it's like this. You, because of your gift, will be put in a position of influence. You can then use that position of influence to further the kingdom of God."

"Peter, I am making sure that Eli is beginning to understand just what I am really doing with him. I am creating probably the best pitcher ever. Because of that, the people that he will be able to touch will be millions."

The pitching coach for the varsity baseball team came to watch Eli play again. He said, "I think it is time to move Eli up to the varsity team."

"You have got to be kidding. He is only eleven years old. You would have to forfeit every game he plays in and screw up his eligibility forever. I won't even approach his mother about this. You scumbag! All you can think about is your own legacy and care nothing for the players!"

The varsity coach walked over to Eli. "Hey, young man! How would you like to pitch at the varsity level?"

"I will have to ask my mom," answered Eli quickly.

Grace came walking up as Eli said he would ask his mom. "Ask me what?"

"If I can pitch for the varsity baseball team."

Grace told Eli to walk to the car. She needed to talk to the coach herself. "Are you out of your mind? How dare you even bring that up to Eli?"

With that, she walked away. Grace went directly to the superintendent's office and filed a complaint with the head of the school. She asked the superintendent for the phone number of the state high school baseball league and called them.

"This is John James with the state high school baseball league."

"Mr. James, the baseball coach from Roseau High just tried to recruit my eleven-year-old son, Eli, to play high school baseball. Is that league policy?"

"Not a chance. Even if he were able to play at that level, he would not have the emotional maturity to play with the older boys."

"Peter, I allowed the coach to do that for one reason and one reason only. I wanted Eli to know that he has the ability, even at this age, to play with anyone," Father stated with the authority that only he commanded.

Grace walked onto the playing field where Eli was warming up. She walked over and gave him a kiss on the cheek.

"Ma! Don't do that in front of my teammates!" a red-faced Eli said.

As she walked away, she had a sly grin on her face.

At practice that day, Eli did slow down his pitches so his teammates could get some quality batting practice. They needed it, as the game they were about to play was a key to their success for the whole season.

Two days later, as they were heading to the field to play the Pirates, Eli stepped away from the rest of his team to throw up.

Eli was nervous. "Mom, this is the first game of the season. What if I totally blow it?"

"You won't," Grace responded quickly.

Arriving at the field, Grace was nervous, but she would not let it show because she knew that Eli would be even more shaken up than he already was if he knew just how nervous she was.

Warming up, Eli started throwing slowly, taking it real easy, as he did not want to throw his arm out. As his arm warmed up, he started to throw faster and faster. Tim Jenkins, the opposing coach, was watching Eli throw. In his mind, he began to wonder how any of his kids could possibly hit Eli.

Eli took his last pitch and started to head for the dugout. Then, just before he stepped off the mound, he thought, *I will throw one with some heat on it just to psyche out the other coach.* He looked at Smitty, his catcher, and gave a nod, and Smitty knew what was coming. He hated it when Eli threw heat. It hurt a lot to catch it. Jenkins happened to look over when Eli let it go. He could hardly see the pitch. Jenkins knew that if Eli threw like that very much in the game, Jenkins's team would lose for sure.

"Pete, watch this game! Eli is going to shine, purely shine!" the Father said.

Since Roseau was the home team, the Pirates were up to bat first. Josh Smith was the first batter up. Three pitches was all it took, and Eli was hardly working. The next batter was Ned Thomson, the best hitter they had. He was a big kid for only being twelve, with a quick bat.

Ned looked out at Eli and yelled at him, "You can't throw fast enough to strike me out."

Smitty called for heat. He hated heat but knew that this guy with the attitude had to go down. Eli nodded and threw the ball at about eighty-five miles an hour. Ned did not even see it. A strike was called. Eli threw the second pitch a little faster. Strike two was called. Eli looked over at his mom. She smiled and knew what he was about to do. Mr. Thomas looked directly at Eli and nodded. Jenkins saw what was going on and had an idea something was up but did not have a clue what it could be. Eli looked in on Smitty and threw a changeup. Ned swung about a half second before the ball got there. Strike three was called. Ned threw the bat in anger. The umpire promptly threw him out of the game.

"Pete! Did I not have Solomon write in Proverbs that pride comes before destruction ? Ned's pride came before his destruction," the Father said.

Eli went to the car after winning the game. "Mom, do you suppose I earned a Blizzard at the DQ?"

"I think you earned that and then some," she responded.

They drove up to the drive-thru, where Eli got his Blizzard.

Their Eyes Meet

Eli was now seventeen. His junior year, up to this point, everything had been going quite well. He had been working really hard. His chest muscles were building and getting harder. His pitches were getting faster and faster. Smitty, his catcher, was able to now handle his fastest balls. They both knew that conditioning was going to be the key to the whole thing.

"Peter, see that cute little thing I created over there?" Father asked with a sly grin on his face.

"I see her, Father. What's your plan?"

"She's mine. She's been my mine for a number of years. She will be an undying fan. She will draw Eli to me," Father responded with love and caring in his voice.

Eli walked into the gym to work out and looked over at the bleachers and stops. He can't believe what he was seeing. Jill was the cutest girl in the school. She kept looking over at him. She smiled, her eyes glimmering in the light. Eli got a bit flustered. A girl had never liked him before. Jill walked up to him, smiled, and started to talk ever so gently to Eli. Grace, watching, started to feel some concern at the whole prospect. Eli walked over to where his mom was.

Eli's mom said, "Eli, the only thing I am going to tell you is to have fun but be careful."

"Mom, she wants me to go to church with her tonight."

Grace thought to herself, *This should be good.*

The next day, when Eli got to the school, he no more than got in the door than Jill *was* there to meet him.

Jill said," Last night at church, you accepted Christ. Do you understand what that is going to mean? Your game is going to get even better. God will give you the strength you need to throw faster and faster."

Father said to Pete, "There is going to be a whole lot more than his pitching getting better and faster."

Pete asked, "What do you mean?"

Father answered, "Watch and see."

Eli went to practice early. He walked into the weight room and started lifting, pushing harder and harder. Jill jumped on the machine right next to Eli and started working as hard as Eli was. The machines were moving faster and faster. The kids were getting stronger and stronger.

Eli could hardly wait until the start of the season. Jill was excited at the prospect of her new boyfriend, the starting pitcher for the Roseau, Lakeview Lions.

Eli's first practice was just around the corner. Eli walked over to the mound, where his speed of ninety-five miles an hour was going to be put to the test, as were the hitters on the squad. The baseball team has learned if they want a good batting practice, they won't give Eli a hard time. Eli suggested they use the batting machine because he wanted to throw his pitches with uniformity.

The coach brought three of the best hitters from the senior class. Eli walked to the mound. He tossed the ball up and caught it. He looked up to heaven and prayed for the three hitters. Then he prayed for where the ball had to go. The biggest bull on the team came to bat first looked at Eli, who was slender and small, Eli smiled to himself. He tossed the ball, took his stance on the mound, wound up, and threw the ball at ninety-eight miles per hour. The bull swung away and did not even come close. On the second pitch, he swung again. Eli looked at Smitty for a call for the changeup. Smitty called for a fastball. Eli shook off the call. He threw the changeup, and the bull drove the ball out of the park. Eli looked over at the coach. He was not happy. The next batter who came to bat was Tim McCaw.

Eli thought to himself, *If I throw nothing but heat, no one can hit me.*

Eli's coach realized that his young pitcher, Eli, just wanted to strike out all of his teammates.

Jill *was* standing on the sidelines, praying, *Father, settle Eli down. Lord, please give him a teachable spirit.*

"Pete, I think it is time to show Eli that he is not great without me. Watch this settle him down. He has got to learn to listen to his coach and to his catcher and, of course, to me."

The next three batters that came up were able to hit Eli out of the park. With every pitch, Eli became more and more frustrated. Every hit made him doubt his ability.

"I have not stunk this bad since I pitched in Little League," he said as he stormed off the mound.

Eli's coach grabbed him by the collar and said, "Listen, kid. If every time something goes bad, you are ready to give up, what good is it? I think it's about time you stop and pray and figure out what God is trying to show you."

"Trying to show me?" Eli *asked*, puzzled. "Coach, you are not supposed to talk to me about God. This is a public school, remember?"

Eli's coach simply asked Eli. "What is the name of your school? You're here so you can talk about Christ."

"Besides Eli, I don't give a flying hoot about the Supreme Court. If I lose my job, so be it. Your future looks really great if you will just let Christ control your life. Eli, listen. You have to let Christ control your actions." He said.

"Let Christ control my life. How do I do that? How do I do it?" In the locker room, Eli sat in a corner by himself. Eli put his face in his hands and looked at the floor. He stood up, grabbed a baseball, and threw it as hard as he could. *Bang!* It punched a hole in the locker. Eli walked over and saw the hole. His eyes got big.

Wow! I did that?

He looked down at his hand, made a fist, and relaxed it. He made another fist. He opened his fist, spread his fingers, and smiled.

Eli walked over to the coach and said, "Let's get 'er done."

The next morning, the alarm went off at 6:00 a.m. Eli rubbed his eyes and crawled out ofbed. He walked downstairs.

Grace looked at him and smiled. "Game day. Are you ready?"

Eli smiled, just smiled. He whistled as he walked out the door, got in the car, and headed to school.

All through the day, the kids gave Eli encouragement. He just felt like praying all day.

Jill saw Eli across the hall and ran over to him. "Eli, you look different. What is going on?"

Jill, I've got to keep my head on this game. Can we talk about it later?" Eli stated.

With that, Jill shrugged her shoulders and walked away.

The day seemed to last three weeks. Finally, the bell rang at 3:19 p.m., and Eli couldn't get to the locker room quickly enough. He walked in, his confidence apparent to everyone there. He tossed the ball up and caught it several times. This was his first varsity game. His nerves were on edge.

The Lions took the field to warm up. Eli was throwing lightly while the coach was giving infield warm-ups to his team. The coach made it clear to Eli that he wanted no heat on the ball.

"Pete! This is going to be fun. The speed Eli will be throwing that ball at is going to be amazing. Eli will have colleges looking at him tonight, and you are about to see what can happen when I give raw gifts to people and they worked their tails off to perfect their gifts.

The crowds were going nuts. The teams huddled.

The coach looked at his team and said, "Okay. Guys, you know what we have been working on for the past three weeks in practice. Keep in mind that if Eli throws one of his fastballs and they connect with it, start running back. It's going deep. Also, be looking for weird hits from his other pitches. When he throws that reverse changeup, that ball does some strange things if they get a piece of it. It usually goes foul, but watch it."

The Lions took the field. Eli walked to the mound. The Bulldogs' best hitter, Todd Johnson, came up to bat first. Their coach had decided to try to shake Eli's confidence early. Eli looked over at his coach and then to his catcher. He got the signal for heat. Eli got a little grin on his face and threw the first fastball of his varsity career. Johnson barely saw it and was not able to even get his bat around. A strike was called. Eli winked at Johnson. Todd started to get angry, which was exactly what Eli wanted. When the opposing batter was not cool, strikeouts were easier to get. Eli tossed the ball and caught it again and again. Eli looked for the signal. Heat again. Heat happens fast. Another strike is called.

Eli thought to himself, *Who's gonna get psyched out here?*

The next signal is for a curve, low and inside. Eli nodded, and Todd *saw* it coming, but the ball dropped so quickly that he could not get close to it. Todd Johnson was called out on strikes. Eli looked over to the Bulldogs' dugout and smiled. He knew he had them right where he wanted them.

The second batter, Randy Smith, came to bat. Randy was a huge guy. He was six feet six inches tall. Randy was so muscular that the school had to spend an extra $500 to be able to put a uniform on him. In his senior year, he expected to get picked up by the pros right after graduation. He had reflexes like a cat. His bat came around like lightning. Eli took his cap off, ran his hands through his hair, looked over at his mom, and smiled.

Eli's coach signaled Eli to walk him.

The expression on Eli's face said it all. He shakes his head, *No way!*

The nonverbal communication to the coach was clear. The coach signals timeout to the catcher, who called timeout to the umpire.

As the coach stormed out to the mound, Eli knew he was in big trouble. "Coach, I can get this guy. I know I can get this guy," Eli stated emphatically.

"Listen, son. Here is the plan. Throw walk pitches on the first two pitches. But throw them hard. The then the third pitch, put it in hard. Let's see what he can do with it. Now look angry, like you are really mad at me. I just made you do something you really don't want to do."

Eli stormed back to the mound. He acted angry to fool the batter. He threw the first two pitches wide so that balls are called. He looked at the catcher. The signal is given. He threw a ninety-mile-per-hour fastball. It totally caught Smith off guard. Strike one is called. The look on Smith's face was priceless. Smith dug in. His cleats threw dirt back at the catcher.

The look in Smith's eyes tells Eli, *You got lucky on that one. It won't happen again.*

Father looked at Peter. "Pete, I am going to give Eli a little more incentive here. Watch this."

Suddenly, Eli heard Jill's sweet voice.

"C'mon, Eli! Smoke him!"

Eli smiled. He did not even look at Jill. He turned his back on Smith, tossed the ball and caught it. Then he turned back to Smith. He threw another ninety-mile-per-hour fastball. Smith did not even get his bat around.

"Strike two!" the umpire yelled.

Smith shook his head. He was getting really angry with himself. This is again just where Eli wanted him. Smitty signaled for a changeup. Eli smiled, looked at his mom, and winked. She knew what was coming. Eli wound up hard. Smith was expecting another fastball. The ball came in at thirty-five mph instead of ninety. Smith swung one half second early. Strike three was the called. Eli grinned. The game was over. Smiles and high-fives abounded as the team congratulated each other. Jill ran out on the field, gave Eli a huge hug, and said, "You played a great game, mister, but to be honest, you really need a shower."

Eli walked to the locker room with the rest of the team. Eli came out of the shower, dressed, and heard one of his buddies say, "Hey, Eli! There's a babe out there waiting for ya."

Smiling, Eli walked out, trying not to look too excited, and said, "Hey, Jill. What's up?"

"Eli!" Jill said. "There's a youth meeting at my church tonight. Care to join me?"

Eli looked into Jill's big, blue eyes and melted. "I would love to. What time and where?" Eli asked.

The smile Jill flashed at Eli, the way she wrinkled her nose made Eli's knees weak. "Can you pick me up at 7:00?" Jill cooed.

Eli's response was instant. "Of course.

The time was now five thirty. Jill rushed home to spend the next hour and a half just getting ready for her new best friend to pick her up. At seven o'clock sharp, Eli drove up in his new Dodge Challenger. The deep purple metallic paint glistened in the moon light. Eli got out of the car and bounded up front steps unto the deck. He knocked on the door and Jill's dad opened it. Eli swallowed hard. "Hello, sir," was all Eli could say.

Jill's dad simply said, "Have her home early."

"Yes sir. Thank you, sir," was all Eli could muster for an answer.

Jill came bouncing out of the house. She looked at her dad, who gave one of those smiles that said, "I got him. I trust you." Jill understood something had happened. She did not know what exactly. But she knew something had happened. All she could do was give him a look that said, "Daddy, you better not have beat him up too bad."

Her dad knew that look and simply said. "He's okay. Just shook him up a little."

With that, off Eli and Jill went to the youth group meeting together.

Peter looked at Father. "Guess you called that one right."

"Pete, when have I ever been wrong? Watch what comes next."

John Crankebaker, the youth leader, was there to meet them.

"Aren't you Eli McBrien?" he asked.

Eli looked over at Jill, who said, "Guess your fame is preceding you."

"Eli, let's do this," John said. John walked over to the stage. "I heard you play a pretty mean guitar."

Eli looked at Jill and asked, "Who told you that?"

Jill smiled as her hair glistened in the bright lights of the gym. "Eli, I just thought you might want to show off some more of your talents. There is more to life than baseball, you know."

Eli got a sly grin on his face.

"Pete, now you are going to see Eli flirt in a way only he can, being humble, yet at the same time, his ego was going to come through in a way that is going to have people wondering what is so special about this kid." The great I am stated with the wonder of the one who created them both.

Eli winked and said, "You know baseball is my gift. This guitar, that's just something I do to ease the tension."

Jill batted her eyelashes and said, "Eli, you know as well as I do that Father gave some people more than one gift. When Father gives us gifts, we have an obligation to use those gifts to build Father's kingdom."

"Okay. You got it."

With that, Eli hopped up onto the stage. The picking runs he did and the total mastery of the guitar he showed had the kids totally awestruck. He smiled at Jill with that sheepish grin. He joined the group and helped lead worship for a while.

John asked, "Eli, are you a believer? I think you must be to get into worship that way."

"Yeah! Isn't everybody?" he answered.

Jill gave him a bit of a frown. "He's Catholic!"

With that, Eli looked at her and said, "The Catholic church is a Christian denomination, is it not? I believe that my sins were paid for on the cross, just like yours."

John piped in, "Wait a minute, you two. In the lesson tonight, we looked at some things that showed what it really means to be a believer. But I set the ground rules a long time ago. We will not attack another church's doctrine here. This is a place for helping build relationships with Christ. Christ will show a person where He wants them, not us."

With that, Jill smiled at Eli. "Guess you win this one."

"No, Jill! The real winner is Jesus Christ! We are here only to serve Him," Eli said.

"Hey, Eli! Could you show me those runs you did?" Hank Smith asked him.

Peter looked over at Father. "Is Jill who you have planned for Eli?"

"Now, Pete, you know that information is not something I am going to share with you. Where would the mystery be? Where would the adventure be if I let you know everything I had in mind? Just stay tuned. You will find out when the time is right."

The Flaming Sword

"Hey, Pete! Watch him take off now. Not only does Eli have his mom pushing him and his natural drive that I have instilled in him; now he will be constantly working to impress Jill. I am so good at this sort of thing. Check this out! I have had the LA scouts watching him for a year, and the phone calls start today."

Eli dragged himself out of bed. He was out late the night before with Jill but knew he had to pay the price if he wanted to achieve the success that people have been telling him he has the potential for.

Anya yelled, "Eli, phone!"

Dragging himself down the stairs, he answered with, "Yeah! What do you want?"

"Eli, this is Morton Smith. I am a scout for Los Angeles."

"Yeah right. Tell me another one," Eli disrespectfully responded.

"Listen Eli. This is not a prank. We have had scouts out at your last seven games, and we are very impressed, especially with your fastball and your changeup. We even were able to sneak a radar gun into the field and clocked your fastball at ninety-two mph. We would like your permission to contact your coach. We might have some ideas that will help improve your fastball. We cannot give you any coaching at this point, as we don't want to have an adverse affect on your amateur status. Eli, we would like to meet with you after your senior season. We are sending information to your mom so she can start communicating with us on your behalf. This is the only direct communication we will have with you, as we are bound by amateur rules as well. High school years are too important for us to screw up just to win some ball games," Smith said.

"Pete, I have just started the ball rolling. Watch for Eli's fame to grow and grow and for everyone to see it. I am going to use Eli to show the world just how powerful I really am. From time to time, I will do things to keep his pride in check." Father's excitement came through to Peter in his expressions.

"Father, how are you going to do that? How are you going to be able to keep his pride in check?" Peter responded.

Father answered, "He is going to have to work his tail off. He will think it's all because of his accomplishments. The answer to that one is Jill. One little word from her, here or there, and he will be brought back to earth. Then his mind will return to Me."

"Of course you can have my permission to talk to my mom," Eli said. "I think I know where this is going. It is gonna be a fun ride."

"Eli, it's going to be fun, but—"

Eli cut in, "I know, Mr. Smith. I know it's gonna be a lot of hard work. Work I'm not scared of. Let's just get the process started."

"Good-bye, Eli." With that, Morton hung up.

Immediately, Morton called Grace back on her cell. "Eli's gave us permission to work it the way we need to. I am having my pitching coaches contact his coach next week. I am sending him some videos and also some diagrams of exercises that are needed in the off season for Eli to increase his speed and control of his pitches."

Grace answered, "I don't really understand the physics of all this, but you send us the information. I will get it to his coaches and work together with them to see that Eli accomplishes what he needs to, to be the best pitcher he can be."

Eli was eating his breakfast when his sister Anya yelled at him again. "Eli, phone! It's Jill."

"Hi, Jill. What's up?"

"Eli, are you up for some fun this Saturday morning?"

"Okay. What did you have in mind?" Eli answered.

"Some of us were going to drive out to Jayne's family's cabin and cruise on their pontoon boat for a while. We will have a campfire and sing some songs. You up for it?" Jill asked.

"Sounds great!"

Ten minutes later, Eli came out of the shower. "Mom, Jill and I are going to Jayne's family's cabin. We are gonna hang out here, sing around a campfire, that sort of thing."

"Pete, I need six angels on this one. I can see now that these kids of mine are going to get involved in some very dangerous activity. They need maximum protection."

"Father, what are they going to get involved with?" Pete asks.

"Peter, I know it was centuries ago, but remember when you were sixteen?" Father responded.

"Oh yeah! I remember," Pete said.

Suddenly, there is a flurry of activity. Angels were coming out from all over. They were being sent by Peter, James, and John to go to earth to protect Eli, Jill, and the rest of the kids from themselves.

Eli's dad had purchased a new Challenger for Eli for his seventeenth birthday. Eli's dad had always loved him, but he just wasn't able to really show it.

Driving up to Jill's house, Eli hopped out, ran up to the door, and asked, "Ready to go?"

"Yes. Let's get rolling. This is sure a nice car your dad bought you for your birthday ," Jill Responded

"My dad, he likes to spend money. He is not there for much else, but he does like to spend money on me," Eli answered with a new voice of caring.

"Father, how is it that Eli has had no earthly Father involved with his life, yet he has totally focused on you and your kingdom?"

"Pete, remember the friend? He has been a quiet influence on Eli's life for years with a word here and there, just enough for me to keep my spirit in front of him. There is also Eli's godly mother. I used both of them. Eli's dad, well, I am still working on him. That will take a little more work, but I will get him too. Remember, a man can run away from that which he knows is right for so long. Sooner or later, it will catch up with him. Then when he does not know which way to turn, that leaves him one way to look, and I am always there," Father said.

"Eli, take me for a ride, would you?" Jill asked, batting her eyelashes at Eli. One could almost see Eli's heart skip a beat. at that.

"Come on! Let's go!" Eli answered.

They hopped in the car and headed off.

Eli asked, "Where do you want to go, sweetheart?"

"Let's head over to the cove at Smithville." *Jill answered with a tenderness that was so warm that if there was any coldness in any heart within hearing distance that heart would be warmed.*

Again, those deep, blue eyes that Jill had caught Eli. He kept driving the car, trying to not look at Jill sitting beside him.

As they reached the cove. Eli got out of the Challenger walked around and opened Jill's door. They walked from the parking lot to the lake and sat in the sand. There was a warm breeze blowing off the water in the cove. The air had a sweet smell to it. Eli put his arm around Jill. She snuggled up to him, and he looked at her angelic face, kissed her forehead, and stopped cold.

"I can't do this," Eli said.

"Do what?"

"I was going to try to make out with you. I just saw the strangest thing I have ever seen in my life."

"Oh," Jill answered.

"As I was about to kiss you, there was fire coming from a sword."

"What?" asked Jill, puzzled.

"Really! Fire from a sword," Eli answered.

"That gets them every time, Pete!" Father stated with glee.

"Father, that had to scare Eli half to death," Pete responded.

"Better halfway than both of them lose their innocence in a few moments of passion!" The great I AM explained.

"Eli, do you think we should head back to the party?" Jill asked.

"You know, I really do. I think we are on very dangerous ground here." Eli said.

They walked back to the Challenger, got in, hardly looking at each other, and then…

"Look, Jill. We have nothing to be ashamed of here. Father has shown us the purity he wants in this relationship, and that's what He is going to get. I care about you *a* lot! I will not give up on that. You are so important to me."

Eli pulled the car over and prayed, *Father, show me if this is what you want.* "Jill, will you wear my class ring?"

"Eli, I can't say yes to that right now. I need to pray about it, but I will wear your letter jacket for a while. I'm cold," Jill said.

Eli smiled a big grin, teeth shining in the dark, and gave Jill a huge hug. He turned back to facing the road. He slid the car into gear. In his excitement, he pushed his foot to the floor. Gravel rocks started to get thrown all over. When the tires hit the pavement, there was a scream as rubber burned on the pavement with the absolute power of the Challenger's Hemi V8.

Eli released the gas pedal and got a sheepish grin on his face. He looked over at Jill. Her face was white with fear.

"Eli, this car has a lot of power. Are you sure you should be driving it?" Jill said.

"Believe me, Jill. With that little burst, I think I learned that this car has way too much power for anyone." Eli responded.

Peter raised a question. "Father, is that car safe for Eli to be driving?"

"Peter, see that patrol car just up the road a mile? Eli is going about ten miles an hour over the speed limit. He's about to get his first ticket." The Father responded.

Eli took his Challenger from third to fourth, stepped on it, felt the power surge, and then saw the lights flash on behind him, followed by a quick siren. "Oh no!" Eli said as he pulled over.

The officer was someone his mom knew. He approached the car slowly, he looked it over with extreme caution, shined his light in the window, and said, "Eli McBrien, does your mom know you are driving this car?"

"Yes. It was a birthday present from my dad," Eli responded.

"Well, young man, you just got your first speeding ticket with it. On top of that, I saw the way you started out back there. I think I just might throw on top of that an exhibitionist driving charge. If I could prove it, I would charge you with hugging the wrong curve," the officer said with a grin.

"Come on, John. You know my mom will kill me if I get these tickets my first night out with this car. What do you mean hugging the wrong curve? This road is completely straight. You mean…I had both hands on the wheel."

"Eli, you were trying to hold my hand!" Jill said with a sly grin.

Eli dropped his head on the steering wheel. "Eli, don't worry. We have no such ticket, although I could figure out something if I wanted to. Just be warned. I am going to nail you for every little thing with this car."

"John, what kind of friend are you?" Eli asked.

"A good one," said the officer quickly.

"Father, that was funny. That was really funny," Peter said, laughing.

"I know. Sometimes I crack myself up with some of the learning situations I put people in," Father said, chuckling.

John gave Eli's mom a call from his squad car. "Grace, I just busted Eli for doing ten over. I let him off on the exhibitionist driving charge, as I think he did not realize the power in his car. I am going to lose the ticket, however, as I don't want this to go on his record."

"Thanks, John. He is a good kid. I think I am going to have a little fun with this," his mom answered.

"Pete, that policeman is doing something he is not supposed to do. I am going to put the thought across Grace's mind to call him back," Father stated emphatically.

"John, sorry to call you back so quickly, but you must do your job. What the judge does is up to him. Eli has to learn to respect that car. This will be a good lesson for him." Grace said.

"Okay, Grace, we'll play it your way," John answered with a questioning tone.

Eli and Jill headed back to the party. Just as they drove up to the church, his phone rang.

"Oh no. It's Mom. I bet John called her! Uh…hi, Mom," Eli answered sheepishly.

"Eli, you better have a good explanation for the kind of driving you have been involved with tonight," Grace stated with a voice that could scare even the toughest angel.

"Mom, the tires were an accident. I also did not realize I was over the speed limit. I hate this car. Why did Dad want to buy me this fancy of a car?" Eli stated.

"Eli, you know as well as I do that he won't be involved with your life in any way except to buy you things, so he spends gobs of money on you," Grace retorted.

"Peter, let's look at this. This kid has a car that most kids his age would give their eyeteeth for. I am going to put it on his heart to do something special with this car. Watch this!"

"Eli! Why don't we go to Roseau? The kids at the grade school all know who you are. They want to be close to you. We need to think up a contest. The winner gets to go with you for a day to see Minneapolis play, and you will take them in your car." Jill Said.

"Jill, that's a great idea!" Eli grabbed the phone to call his coach.

"Pete, see what my spirit will do. It is constantly looking for ways to build the reputation of my kids that allows them to speak into the lives of those around them." Father said.

"Okay, Coach. How are we going to do this? You say there is a camp coming up in May for all the young kids. But how do we choose who improves the most? How do we pick one kid to receive this award?" Eli said.

"Eli, I think that we just have to be able to not pick the most improved, per se. We pick the kid who works the hardest to improve what he has. By doing the award that way, we are going to build the kids' confidence and also will build your reputation with the pros." His coach responded.

"Coach, I couldn't care less about my reputation with the pros. I am about helping the young kids be all they can be. But the other thing I need is to hit the press with what I am going to be doing for these kids so we can get the cops off my case. I am not trying to break laws. All I was trying to do was what was best for the kids as well as trying to enjoy my last year of school," Eli said.

On Monday, the announcement went out over the school's intercom that grades four through six, boys and girls, would have a chance to play ball with the greatest baseball player ever to come out of Roseau, Eli McBrien. He was going to be putting on a clinic the next three Saturdays. Then an announcement came that there was going to be a special award involved for one category of player. That category is going to be announced by Eli and his coach only after the player has achieved what it takes to win the special award.

"Pete, see that little Tommy Smith. He has a head as big as a globe. He thinks because I have given him lots of raw talent he can conquer everything and win everything.

The big problem is that he is lazy. I am going to cure that. Someday, he will serve me too!" the Great I Am said.

Saturday arrived. Eli was driving his Challenger to practice, and the lights went on.

"Oh no! Now what did I do now?"

"Morning, Eli," John said.

Eli answered quickly, "John, what did I do? I was driving under the speed limit, and I signaled for all my turns. What did I do?"

"Relax, Eli," John responded. "I am just telling you how proud I am to know you. What you are doing for these kids is great. Can you give me a hint on what it will take to win that award?"

"John your kid is going to be there today and the next three weeks. I can't do that. It would not be fair to the rest of the kids," Eli answered with an intense tone in his voice.

"Father, you really have instilled integrity into Eli. He knows what he is going to do and how it works," Pete said.

"Pete, you have not seen anything yet. All of his hard work is going to pay some huge dividends over the next few years. Just watch what I am about to do," the great I AM answered.

As Eli turned the corner into the ballpark, he could hardly believe his eyes. "There must be a hundred kids here!" He thought. As he got out of his car, he looked at the mass of young ball players and prayed, "Father, show me the one through all of them you are going to use me to really touch."

Tommy pushed his way through to Eli and said. "You might as well just give me the award now. There is no one here who can beat me at anything."

Eli smiled at Tommy. "Pride comes before destruction, according to Proverbs. Work hard, and you might win the award."

"Might! I can win anything that you put up without even trying. Just watch me," Tommy said as Eli shook his head as he walked away.

"Okay. Pitchers and infielders over here. Outfielders over there," Eli ordered.

Eli walked over to work with the pitchers while John Thomas worked with the infielders.

Tommy insisted on pitching first, but Eli selected a boy who was skinny with horn-rimmed glasses to go first.

"Pete, see that little boy. His name is Aaron Bursa. He does not have a lot of confidence yet, but just watch what I am going to do with him over the years. I believe in taking the last and making them first," The Father said.

Through the day, Eli watched all the kids. Some worked really hard, and some just use their natural talent. Eli kept noticing the boy in the horn-rimmed glasses. Eli walked over to him, put his hand on his shoulder, took the ball, and showed him the proper way to hold the ball.

Just then, Tommy pushed in and said, "Don't waste your time with Aaron. He is a loser!"

The answer came back quickly. "Tommy, you are done. Take your glove and go home! If your mom or dad want to talk to me, they can call me."

The stunned look on Tommy's face was priceless.

"But I'm the best. You can't do that," Tommy said.

"Tommy, your arrogance and pride are an example of sportsmanship that no one needs to learn. They need to see it for the bad behavior it is. I don't care what your natural talents are. I will not tolerate such behavior. You're outta here!" Eli stated very intensely as he walked away from Tommy.

The next practice, all the kids showed up, even Tommy with his dad in tow.

"How dare you kick Tommy out! He is the best pitcher here, and you know it," John said.

Eli realized that this was more than he bargained for. "Look, John this is about helping kids. Having Tommy putting down the kids who are working their butts off because he was blessed with more natural talent is not acceptable. I don't want him here," Eli stated.

John looked at Tommy. "Young man, head for the car. If there is one thing I know about Eli, he is a man who tells the truth. You are going to learn what it means to be a sportsman and also that messing up has penalties. Thanks, Eli. We will talk later," John said as he walked away.

"Okay, John. Later," Eli responded.

John grabbed Tommy by the ear, just about lifted him off the ground, and dragged him to the car.

"Pete! I have just hit a homerun. Tommy was going to learn a lesson here that he will remember for the rest of his life, and his bottom won't be the same for a week," Father said with a smile.

At the end of three weeks of practice, the time had come to make the choice. Which kid would Eli take to the game? He looked at all the kids. They had all worked hard.

Eli looked up and asked, "Whom, Father? Whom?" The words came out of his mouth just like water. "Aaron Bursa, let's go to a game in Minneapolis next week."

The smile on Aaron's face could have lit up the Minneapolis stadium.

"Really?" Aaron responded. Aaron had not had a great deal of success in his life. But that was about to change forever with this trip to one ballgame.

"Yes, I think you worked the hardest. It was a really hard choice, but you made it," Eli, smiling, said.

Jill, standing on the sidelines, smiled. She saw things in Eli that she knew were going to make him a great player and a great husband and father someday. As Eli walked off the field, Jill was waiting for him and threw her arms around his neck.

"Eli, what you did for these kids was great!" Eli took her hand and guided her to the Challenger. He opened her door and kissed her on the forehead.

Aaron's Big Day

It was mid-May. Eli once again dragged himself out of bed and down the stairs and poured himself a cup of coffee. "Eli, you don't drink coffee," Eli's mom said.

"Mom, it was a late night last night. After the concert, all the kids wanted to go get malts at the DQ, so we did. We closed up the place, got the kids home, and then I drove Jill home around one a.m. Oh, and one other thing. Jill's dad is going to call you, something about me keeping her out too late."

"Eli, he already did. We are going to have a joint meeting with Jill, you, me, and her parents."

"Oh boy! This ought to be good. Mom, nothing happened. We were with other kids all night," Eli said in a very tired voice.

"Eli, it does not matter. You have to honor her and her parents," Grace responded.

"Gotcha! Where's that number? Where is that number?"

"Eli, what number?"

"Aaron's," Eli said very impatiently.

"Right here. What are you going to do with that?" his mom responded.

"Mom, I promised him a game. Remember? I have to keep my word. I had the coach get me some tickets to the game this week when Minneapolis plays Chicago. Todd Rucket is making the pitchers everywhere look sick. I gotta see this guy. I wonder if I could beat him. I think it would be a fun time with the kid," Eli stated with a voice that is waking more and more.

With that, Eli picked up the phone and dialed. "Hello, Mrs. Bursa. This is Eli McBrien. I picked up some tickets right behind the dugout . When Aaron and I get to the game, he can see everything. Todd Rucket will be playing for Minnesota in this game. I want to start showing Aaron what the big leagues are really about."

"Eli, you have to promise me one thing," Aaron's mom said.

"What's that, Mrs. Bursa?" Eli responded.

"Eli, you can't drive over the speed limit," she said with a tone of authority.

"Mrs. Bursa, did you hear about the first time I drove the Challenger?" Eli asked.

"Eli, the whole town did," she said.

"I promise, no speeding," Eli promised.

"Aaron telephone It's Eli McBrien," Mrs. Bursa said to Aaron.

"Hi Eli. This is great. You really called me," Aaron said.

"Settle down, Aaron. I promised you a game, and this one is going to be a real treat. Chicago is in town to play Minneapolis next Friday. I realized that we would still be in school. But what do you say we cut out before the last hour and take a trip to Minneapolis and catch the game?" Eli asked with enthusiasm in his voice.

"Ma!"

"Aaron, I have already spoken with Mrs. Harris, the principal. And yes, you can go," Mrs. Bursa excitedly said.

Aaron became so excited he started jumping all over the place. On the couch, over to the chair, and back to the couch. "Yes!" he yelled, raising his fist in the air. His hands went up in victory.

"Whoa, champ. You are going to a ball game. Not the World Series!" Aaron's mother said, smiling.

"Pete, you look as excited at all of this as Aaron does. Aaron's mother did not understand the implications of her statement. But she will in due time."

"Father, what are you doing here between Aaron and Eli?" Pete asked.

"Pete, the friendship is going to have huge implications for Aaron. The whole team is going to be looking up to him when he gets to be Eli's age. He will never be at Eli's level, but he will be a great high school pitcher," the Father stated.

Arriving at the ballpark, Aaron's eyes got as big as saucers. "Wow, Eli! Thanks for bringing me. This is awesome!" The excitement in his voice made him squeak.

"Aaron, you earned this. You were the hardest-working guy out there."

Eli and Aaron walked up and found their seats right behind Minnesota's dugout. Eli took the time to explain what he looked for in batters as he watched them warm up.

"Look over here at Rucket. Notice he stands just a bit differently as he is warming up for how and where he intends to hit the ball. If he wants to hit a long ball, his feet are just a bit wider. But if he wants to drive it to left or right, his left foot takes a different spot in the box. Most guys don't study hitters. They just try to fool them. If you watch how they hit, then you can figure out what they are trying to do. Once you figure out what they are trying to do, then you know what kind of ball you can give them to keep them from accomplishing their task," Eli said.

Aaron was totally fixated on every word that Eli was telling him.

"Every time Rucket comes up to bat, I want you to try to guess where he is going to try to drive the ball. Rucket is a master of the art of hitting. There are very few pitchers that can actually beat him. Some get lucky, but few beat him," Eli said with an instructive tone in his voice.

"Peter, the friendship that is building here will never end. When the time comes for me to bring Eli home, Aaron will be at his bedside. I am setting Aaron up to coach. He will be a great one. The reason he is going to be a great coach is because of the time he spends with Eli now," Father stated in his most loving tone.

"So what you are telling me, Father, is a person's future can be determined by one taking a kid under their wing, so to speak, and helping that kid? In doing so, we are helping that young person years down the line, when he or she is an adult? The things that are shared now, that are learned as a kid, come back to mind as an adult?" Peter asked.

"Pete, you got it. You really do. Now, do you understand why my Son became so upset with you when he told you to let the little ones come to me, for such is the kingdom of heaven?" Father stated.

"Got it, Father," Peter responded.

Aaron ate three hot dogs, drank two sodas, went to the men's room three times to get rid of the sodas, and about broke Eli.

Eli smiled to himself. *Boy, having kids will be expensive. If I can have kids as great as this one, it will be worth it*, Eli thought to himself.

Minnesota won 4 to 3. Rucket saved the game in the bottom of the ninth with a two-run homer.

"Aaron, the pitcher tried to fool Rucket. A hitter that great can't be fooled. A pitcher has to have confidence enough in his throwing to be able to come with his best pitch. This guy did not," Eli stated as a teacher to a pupil.

"Eli, what would you have thrown?" Aaron asked.

"My fastball, of course. At this point, he would have hit me. Give me a couple more years and he would not have seen it," Eli stated with confidence.

Back in the car, Aaron asked, "Eli, would you squeal the tires for me?"

"Sorry, bud. Last time I did it, I was not even trying and ended up with a ticket," Eli responded.

Eli noticed that Aaron was falling asleep as he drove back to Roseau.

"Hey, dude, fold down your seat. If you sleep, that's fine with me."

Six hours later, they pull up to the Bursas' house.

Aaron's mom came to the car. "He's out, I see," she said.

"Yeah, but he had fun. Boy, could that kid eat!" A very tired Eli said.

Eli helped get Aaron into the house, said good-bye to his mom and dad, and cruised just under the speed limit home.

On Monday, Eli's alarm went off. He reached over and shut it off. Grace sent Leah to pound on Eli's door.

"Eli! Get up! You might be famous around town, but here you are still just Eli McBrien. You are not special. Now, get up!" Leah yelled.

Eli crawled out of bed and managed to get himself to the shower and get cleaned up. He brushed his teeth. Then he heard Leah pounding on the bathroom door.

"Hey, pretty boy, Jill is at the door. She says she needs a ride to school. She missed her bus. Again," Leah yelled.

"Good morning, Jill. Heard you missed your bus," Eli said.

"Well, kinda sorta on purpose," Jill responded.

Eli said, "I'm surprised your dad will even let you talk to me after getting you home so late the other night."

Jill responded, "Well, he was a bit upset. But I had him call some of the other parents. They were mad too, but they all did find out we were just cruising and keeping it moral. Then he was okay. Eli, are you going to the soccer game Friday?"

Eli answered, "Jill, no one has asked me yet."

"Eli, I'm asking," Jill responded in her sweetest voice.

"Sure, Jill, I'll go with you. I'll be busy after school all week. Coach wants me lifting and running and lifting. Then he wants me to throw fifty pitches a night," Eli stated, "plus practice."

"Eli, do you know why the coach wants you to work so hard? No one in any school in the state can hit your pitches. Why the extra work?" Jill asked.

Eli took Jill's hand and walked her to the car, opened the door, and smiled.

"Pete, this is where Eli is going to find out if Jill can be trusted. If he tells her and she spills the beans, it could cause the press to come down on Eli in a way he really does not want.

"Okay, Father. Can she be trusted?"

Father just smiled at Peter.

Eli smiled as he looked over at Jill while he was driving down the road toward the school.

Jill looked over at Eli. "Watch the road, buster. You are looking at the wrong curve, as the officer said a few months ago."

"Oh, all right," Eli answered with a smile.

"Are you going to tell me why you are working so hard?"

"Jill, I am working as hard as I am because I want to be the best pitcher I can possibly be."

"Eli, do you trust me?" Jill asked with a somewhat suggestive tone to her voice.

"Of course I trust you," Eli answered with a question in his tone.

"Keep your eyes on the road, not on my legs. Then why won't you tell me?" Jill asked.

Eli pulled into the school parking lot. Just as he pulled in, his coach pounded on his window.

The coach said, "Eli, get your butt into the gym. You have an hour before your next class, and I want you working on the quads."

"Coach, there is more to life than baseball. Today is the gathering around the flagpole sponsored by the Fellowship of Christian Athletes," Eli responded with purpose in his voice.

"Okay. You win. Tomorrow, I want you in the gym," the coach responded.

Eli hopped out of the car, went around and opened the door, took Jill by the hand, and walked over with her to the pole. For the next hour, students stood, prayed, shared, and prayed some more for the next year in school.

"Peter, you see Eli does have his priorities right. He won't compromise on what he knows to be the right thing to do," Father said.

It was a record year for prayer around the pole. They had seventy-five students this year, in large part because of all the time and effort that Eli and Jill had put into getting things ready. They had talked to hundreds of students to get the numbers necessary to show the public that students were still sold out to Christ and His kingdom.

The phone rang. "Hi. This is Grace with Her Highness beauty aids. May I help you?"

"Grace, this is Morton Smith. I hear Eli is shaking things up at school with the Fellowship of Christian Athletes."

"Yes! That's right, and I am proud of him for it."

"Well, as long as this does not take away from the workout schedule we have his coaches working with him on."

"Wait just a minute there, mister! My son is going to get everything he can out of his senior year of high school. If that means he misses some of your practice time so he can devote his time to doing what the Lord would have him do, then you are going to back off. This stuff is as important as any workouts that you could give him. Just ask the coach how hard he works when he does. You won't have to worry a bit. Now back off!" Grace said.

"Father, it looks like Grace has the same values as her son," Pete said.

"I do things right the first time, Pete," is the answer the great I AM gave quickly.

Eli took Jill's hand as they stood with the other students at the flagpole. They continued singing and praying, with all the praise rising with all the others around the country.

Finally, as Jill and Eli started to walk away, Jill thought out loud, "I wonder if they heard all of this in heaven?"

"I will guarantee they did," Eli said.

"I wonder what the angels thought," Jill replied.

"Father, what is going on here? I have never seen the angels dancing this hard. Maybe when your son was born, they danced harder, but why all the excitement?"

"When Eli hits it big, the schools are going to ask him to come in. He will do so with the understanding that he can say what really drives him to be the best he can be. And it won't be the army," was the response with all the pride a Father could have in a son. That's the pride The Father had in Eli.

As Eli and Jill headed into the school for class, Eli reached his arm around Jill's waist.

"Eli, now you are hugging the wrong curve. We don't want to start getting physical at this point. It's too hard to control."

"Yeah, I know, but it feels so good."

"Eli!" Jill stated emphatically.

"Okay, okay," Eli responded sheepishly.

"Pete! Dispatch three angels for each of them. I want twenty-four-hour surveillance on them. They can't make a mistake. There is too much riding on their being an example to all those around them!"

"Gotcha, Father!" Pete responded.

Peter went into the angels' quarters. "I need six of you—Zeke, Thomas, Carlos, Rafael, Luke, and, oh yeah, Thumbnail."

"Me! I am the smallest. I never get called on to do anything. What is it you have for me?"

Peter responded, "I want you to be so close to Eli that you can hear him breathe. If he starts putting his hands where they should not go, you start talking to him in a way that totally breaks his concentration. You don't stop. Just keep talking. He will hear you."

All through the first hour of English class, Jill and Eli kept making eye contact.

Mr. Johnson, the English teacher, noticed it about halfway through the class. "Okay, you two love birds. Time to pay attention or you might find that graduation night does not come this year!"

With that admonition, both Eli and Jill stuck their respective noses in their own books.

Shakespeare's *Romeo and Juliet* all of a sudden took on new meaning for both students. The couple was able to place themselves in the story. Then Mr. Johnson made an announcement that caught both Eli and Jill off guard.

"Students, the play, *Romeo and Juliet*, will be produced by the senior class. I have already cast the lead roles in the play."

Eli looked over at Jill and said "I wonder who that will be?"

"Mr. McBrien, I am going to answer your question right now. It will be you and Miss Thompson."

Eli and Jill looked at each other. Then they realized that they were going to be put in positions that a young couple who are dating should not be in.

"Uh, Mr. Johnson, I don't think that would be such a good idea."

Mr. Johnson replied quickly, "Why not?"

"Mr. Johnson, let me ask, what is involved with the scenes?"

"Talk to me after class," he said.

With that, they went back to work reading the play.

As the bell rang, Mr. Johnson called Jill and Eli to his desk. "Kids, I want to break new ground with this story. The love scene will be somewhat graphic."

"Mr. Johnson, I won't do it," Eli emphatically stated.

"Eli, if I flunk you, you won't play baseball," Mr. Johnson threatened. Eli looked at Jill and saw his future in front of him kind of slipping away. Eli said, "Let us think about it."

Eli and Jill left Mr. Johnson's classroom.

"Jill, this is not over yet. My mom is going to have a royal fit about this. Watch this." Eli dialed Grace's cell number. "Mom, Mr. Johnson, my English teacher, just announced that Jill and I would be doing the lead in *Romeo and Juliet*," Eli said.

"Eli, that's great!" Grace answered.

"Not so fast, Mom," Eli said. "He is planning on breaking new ground. You figure that out. When I told him I would not do it, he threatened to fail me. Then I wouldn't be able to play baseball."

"Eli, give me five minutes. I am coming down."

When Grace stormed into the school, the fumes could almost be seen coming out of her ears. She walked into Mr. Johnson's room and asked him to step outside for a moment.

"Mrs. McBrien, I am trying to teach this class," Johnson said.

"Mr. Johnson, either you come outside the room now or I will tell your students what you have asked Jill and Eli to do. I will go to the principal and we will discuss it with him," is Grace's angry response.

They stepped outside the classroom.

"You will not require those kids to do that play, and you will not flunk Eli for refusing to do it. Is that clear?" Grace's voice could not only be heard in the school but for one block in either direction. Mr. Johnson called Eli and Jill to his desk. "I want to apologize for my actions. I understand your coaches have an offseason workout regime that starts in twenty-five minutes, so I will let you go. Your mother is a great woman! You had better be really grateful for her," Mr. Johnson asked.

As Eli and Jill left the room, Eli turned and said, "Mr. Johnson, I can think of only one better mother. She lived over two thousand years ago." Eli gave Jill a quick hug and headed for practice.

Eli walked out of the locker room, picked up the ball, tossed it a time or two, and throws with power he has never felt before.

"Eli, where did the speed come from?" asked Eli's coach.

"Must be God. I have not been doing anything differently," Eli answered.

"Eli, this is a public school. You know we can't give God credit for anything," the coach stated with a smile, realizing this was the same thing Eli had said to him when he played junior-high ball.

"Listen, Coach. You can say what you want. If I say anything else, I would be lying. Let them throw me in jail for it. Let them kick me off the team. It will make the superintendent of this school look really good as he tries to take away my free speech." With that, Eli threw the next pitch harder and faster than the last. The ball hit the gym wall at about 115 miles an hour.

"Eli, I have never seen pitches at that speed! I had the gun on it. The majors can't throw that fast."

Eli shrugged. He walked over to the water fountain and spit.

"Oh! Eli! Ick!"

Eli looked up. There was Jill.

"Hey, you are not supposed to be in here."

"Eli, I think we should do that play," Jill responded.

"No way! I will not compromise. A ball career is not as important as honoring that which the Lord has shown us to be right. Now, Jill, get out of the locker room!"

Jill stormed out, mad as a wet hen. She wanted to do the play.

"Thumbnail, you are doing a great job. Just keep the words going into Eli's ear so he knows what is right," Father said.

"Gotcha, Most High King,"as Thumbnail started dancing on Eli's shoulder.

Just then, Eli turned the water on for a shower. Father allowed the water to wash Thumbnail off Eli's shoulder with a whoosh. Thumbnail got up out of the water before the drain sucked him under. He looked up and saw the heavenly Father chuckling as Eli grabbed a towel and walked out of the shower room.

"Pete, that was funny. That was really, really funny. But you know what? Thumbnail had to learn not to gloat. He just learned that lesson well." The Father said.

As Eli walked toward his Challenger, he saw three cute cheerleaders from school sitting on the hood.

Thumbnail stated in such a loud voice that the girls could almost hear him, "Eli! get those girls off your car. They are going to wreck your paint job. Don't be nice about it."

"Get off my car now!" Eli yelled.

The girls were shocked by the anger in his voice.

"All right! All right! Don't have a cow! We are getting off. That was sure a mean way to talk to us. At least you could offer us a ride home."

Thumbnail said, "Don't do it!"

"I am truly sorry, ladies. Not tonight," Eli said.

Eli walked over and opened the door, and Janice, a football cheerleader, got in the backseat before he could stop her.

"Now what you gonna do, stud?" she asked.

"Just this." With that, Eli dialed 911. "Hi. This is Eli McBrien. I have a cheerleader in the backseat of my Challenger who will not get out. Can you send a squad car to remove her?"

Bill Smith of the *Roseau Courier* heard the police scanner. "Eli McBrien, what trouble do you have yourself in now?"

John pulls up beside Eli's Challenger. "Eli, buddy, what is the problem here?"

"John, Janice won't get out of my car. She insists that I take her home!"

John puts his arm around Eli. "Eli, now let me get this straight. You have a cute cheerleader in the backseat of your car, and you want *me* to get her out?" John shook his head as he said, "Just give her a ride home."

"John, I care a lot about Jill. I am not going to mess that up" Eli said.

"Okay. Eli, simple solution. Call Jill and ask her to come and ride with you."

"Great idea!" With that, Eli pulled out his cell phone and dialed Jill. "I know you are mad at me, sweetie, but

I have this problem. This is the truth. I came out of the locker room, and there were three cheerleaders—"

"Eli, say no more. I will be there in two minutes."

One minute and twenty-eight seconds later, Jill's dad showed up to drop her off.

"Okay, you guys, who wants to mess with me?" Jill's dad asked.

"Daddy, let Eli and me handle this," Jill responded to her dad.

"That was fun watching Thumbnail jump from Eli to John and back to Eli just to get Jill to show up with her dad," Father said.

Jill stuck her head in the driver's side door. "Jan Smith, how dare you try to force my boyfriend to give you a ride home. Get out of his car now or we will have John here arrest you for all kinds of things."

With that threat, Jan get's out of Eli's Challenger. "Humph! What a bi—"

"Don't say anything you will be sorry for," Jill answered.

Eli opened Jill's door and then walked around and slides in his seat. John walked up to the driver's side," Eli, you know what would really make these girls think you are really upset with them?"

"What's that, John?"

This has positraction, does it not?"

"I think so."

"I am going to get in my car and start to drive off that way." John pointed south. "You step on the brake and hold it while you make your tires scream as you head out of the lot that way." He points north. "Be careful when you release the brake. This thing will about jump out from under you, but you will get the most smoke out of your tires that way," John said.

"Are you sure? All I need is another ticket," Eli responded in a questioning tone.

"Eli, I won't see a thing."

Jill looked over at Eli. Eli was watching for John's car to be headed out of the lot. The cheerleaders started to walk toward the Challenger. Eli stepped on the brake with one foot and stuck his other foot to the floor. The Hemi roared. The car sat still, and blue smoke started to envelop the girls, with blue stinky smoke. All of a sudden, the tires caught, and the Challenger jumped to eighty in the empty parking lot. Eli backed off and got it back under control.

Jill smiled as she said, "It's going to take them months to get the smell of burning rubber out of their clothes, not to mention their hair."

Thumbnail said, "Man, did I pull that one off!"

"Ah, Thumbnail, you better watch that pride. You know what happened the last time."

"Sorry, Father. I just got excited I guess."

"That's okay. Just remember who really gets the credit here and you will do just fine," the Father states emphatically.

Jill smiled at Eli. There was something new in the smile, and there was also a little different look in her eyes. "Eli, I think we should—"

"Jill, we are not going there. I care more about you than you know. But we can't go there."

One could almost see Thumbnail smiling to himself as he thought to himself, *I did good!*

Jill took Eli's hand. "I know now that I can trust you. I feel really safe with you. Most guys, if I had made the offer I made to you, would have taken advantage of the situation."

"Believe me, Jill. It's not because I would not have wanted to. It's because it would not be the right thing to do," Eli responded.

"Father, you have instilled in him values well beyond his years. Will his classmates catch it?" Pete asked.

"Pete, if I told you everything, where would your surprise be?" Father answered with a chuckle.

Eli drove into his mom's driveway, revved the Hemi, shut it down, and walked in the house with a silly grin on his face.

"Hold it right there, buster!" Eli heard his mom say in one of those voices.

Eli thought to himself, *What did I do now?*

"Eli, coming in late like this and revving that car, the neighbors are going to have an uproar."

"Maybe I ought to put a name on the Challenger. Uproar." With that, Eli went to bed.

The Thrill of Victory and Agony of the End

Eli looked around the diamond for the last time. They had just won the state championship. He had just thrown his last pitch as a Lion He was elated yet very depressed. Eli looked in the stands and saw his mom and Jill. Both were smiling and cheering, yet Eli felt sadness, a sadness only those who have had to walk off the field for the last time understand. He reached down, picked a blade of grass, and held it to his nose. He thought to himself, *I just want to remember this smell forever. I want to remember the rest of the team. I want to remember all of the tough spots we got ourselves out of. I just want to remember…* With that he threw the ball up behind his back for the last time in his high school career. He caught it at his waist and walked off the diamond for the last time as a Lion.

Several of the members of the team were going to play college ball. Several teams had contacted him and offered him scholarships to play in college. Eli, however, felt a pull in another direction, a pull that was going to lead him into the greatest adventure a young ballplayer could ever hope for.

“Father, is this the down period before Eli gets the call in the morning from Los Angeles?” Pete asked.

“Yes, Pete. I had to let him feel the joy and sadness. He had to go through all things that a young person does,” Father said.

The next morning, Eli, was still feeling a bit depressed, as he got yelled at by his little sister Leah.

“Eli, why is it always so hard to get you out of bed in the morning? There are two men with fancy cars and, ‘Los Angeles,’ written all over their clothes waiting for you in the living room!” Leah said.

Eli jumped out of bed and dashed downstairs and then realized that he was still in his underwear.

Eli’s mom exploded. “Young man, get yourself upstairs and put some clothes on!” Grace was so embarrassed that her face was three shades of red.

“Pete, that is something the coaches are going to tease him about for years,” Father said.

Eli looked at himself, turned red, and ran back to his room. He came out five minutes later fully clothed.

Jim Ross, the personnel director for the Los Angeles farm club in International Falls, sat across the table from Eli. “Eli, we are prepared to offer you a contract to play with the Crystals.”

The smile on Eli's face lit up the room. "Mr. Ross, I really want to do it. My grandpa always told me to sleep on big decisions before I make them. May I have twenty-four hours? Then we can take the contract to our attorney as well," Eli said.

"Sure, Eli. Not a problem. I will be back in the morning, but we want you pitching tomorrow night if you say yes," Jim stated.

Jim left. Eli gave a hoot and a holler. "Mom, I made it! Give me the contract. I am going to see Stan Smith this morning. I want his opinion on this contract."

Eli burst into Stan's office. His secretary looked at him and said, "Eli McBrien, what brings you here?"

"Well, I have this contract from the Los Angeles farm club. They want me to play baseball for them," Eli answered.

Stan heard Eli in the outer office and quickly came out. "Let me see that young man." Stan read over it quickly and said, "Eli, it's a good contract. You have nothing to worry about here. If you want to play, it simply stated they will pay you a couple hundred bucks a game and they can release you at any time. Also, you could be called up to Los Angeles's major league team at any time."

"Thanks, Stan. What do I owe you?"

"Two tickets to the World Series when you make it."

"You got it!"

Eli ran out to his Challenger, stomped it, and headed back to the house. All of a sudden, the lights behind him came on.

"Shoot!" Eli pulled over.

John, the town policeman, walked up to the car. "Eli, slow down. The news is all over town. I understand the excitement. But just slow down!"

Eli drove home, walked in the house, and told his mom, "The contract is okay. I want to call Dad and see what he thinks." Eli grabbed his cell phone. "Dad, hi. I was just offered a contract with LA's farm team today. What do you think?"

"Eli, it's a waste of time. Do you know how many guys make it to the big time? You ought to just go to school and learn something you can use."

Eli's jaw dropped. He looked at Grace.

She said, "Eli, I knew he would say no. You are young. Play for a couple of years and see where it gets you. You have tremendous talent!"

Eli signed the contract. He spent his last night with his family before he started work with the Crystals.

At 7:00 a.m. the next morning, the doorbell rang. It was Jim Ross. "Eli, are you going to play?" Jim asked.

"Mr. Ross, here is your signed contract," Eli said

"Good! We have a bus to catch," Jim stated with total authority.

Eli quickly threw some clothes in a gym bag and headed for the park. It took them about twenty-five minutes to get to the park, hopped on the bus, and were on their way to St. Paul to face the Saints. Eli had a meal with the team, which felt a lot different than in high school.

His new catcher came up to him. "So, you're the new hotshot we have heard so much about. We have been one pitcher short half the season because they expected you would be coming on. I'm Scott Hogue. I will be catching you. One is a fastball, two a changeup, three a curve, and I tap my thighs for the direction of the ball."

Hank Jones, the team manager, came up to Eli. "I'm starting you tonight. I've been working my pitchers hard, and they all need tonight to rest. These guys have been hitting everyone out of the park. I expect you to be our sacrificial lamb."

Eli thought to himself, *No way!* Eli now had a 103-mile-an-hour fastball, a sinking curve, and a changeup that no one had been able to hit.

Father's glee was evident as he said, "Pete, watch this! I am going to have Eli throw a perfect game his first time out. His next game is going to be humbling, however."

"Father, if he throws a perfect game here, it will catch the attention of the front office," Pete responded.

"Pete, that's the idea," Father replied.

The first guy up was a big boy, six feet five inches tall and 225 pounds.

Eli thought to himself, *This guy should be playing football, not baseball. I hear he hits a lot of homers but has trouble with really fast pitches. I wonder if I can set him up to finish him off with my changeup.*

Scott signaled a curve inside. Eli shook it off. Again, the signal for the curve came. Eli shook it off. The signal came for a fastball. Eli nodded. He let fly a 100-mile per-hour fastball right down the middle. The big guy about spun around he missed it by so much. Again, a signal for a curve came. Again, Eli said no. The catcher signaled for another fastball. Eli nodded and brought the heat. The batter swung around so fast that the bat came out of his hand and headed directly for Eli's head. Eli ducked, picked up the bat, walked it back to the batter, and handed it to him. As he walked back to the mound, he was chuckling to himself. The catcher signaled for another curve. Once again, Eli shook his head no. Then the catcher signaled for a changeup. Eli nodded and threw a changeup that looked to be coming at 100 miles an hour, but in reality it came at 60 miles an hour. The big guy spun around and ended up on the ground from that one.

The rest of the game was very much like the beginning. Eli ended up throwing a perfect game his first time out.

"Pete, Eli is about to experience the temptations that being a pro in sports at any level can put before him. I want six angels around Eli at all times. If anyone besides Jill comes close to him, I want them to see flaming swords!" Father commanded.

"Okay. I need six big angels now!"

Thumbnail is the first one out.

"Not this time," Pete said.

Father responded, "Send him. This will be fun for him!"

"Okay, Father. You are the boss."

"Pete, it would be well for you not to forget that."

"Father, thank you," Peter answered.

"Eli, we're going out for beers. Wanna join us?" Scott asked.

"No thanks, Scott. I'm tired. It's been a busy day. Besides, I'm not much of a drinker," Eli responded.

"Don't worry, buddy. We are gonna change that."

"No. I have a target, and that target does not get hit by my getting drunk out of my mind." With that, Eli stormed off.

Scott, not to be deterred, grabbed Eli by the shoulder. "Then don't drink. Besides, we need a designated driver."

"Okay. Just for a while," Eli responded.

They arrived at Chauncies at about 9:00 p.m. Eli walked to the bar and ordered a Coke.

Chris, the bartender, looked at Eli. "So, you're the great Eli McBrien, I take it."

"That's me."

"Well, Mr. McBrien, let's get together after work and…Oh my God! Oh my God! Look at that flaming sword! Oh my God!" Chris ran over to the other end of the bar, shook her head, and looked back at Eli. She just saw the crowd now.

Next, a beautiful blonde walked up to Eli. "Hey, sport. Buy me a drink. Oh my God! What the—?" She ran out of the bar.

Scott walked up to Eli. "Hey, man. I have never seen chicks react to anyone like they react to you. What are you saying to them?"

"Nothin'. I opened my mouth to say something, and they freaked and ran out," Eli said.

"Man, something is going on. Here comes another babe. Let's see if it happens with her," Scott said.

Eli got up and walked across the room and gave Jill a big hug. Jill looked into Eli's eyes and asked, "Eli, why is there such a sweet, soft light over your head tonight?"

"I don't know. I guess it is because I am really that sweet. Come on, hon. Let's blow this joint and go have some fun." Eli took Jill by the hand, walked out to the car, gunned it, and drove off.

Cruising down Route 53 toward Superior, Eli suddenly saw the lights of a highway patrol car flying up behind him.

"Shoot! I am not speeding!"

Eli pulled over, and the highway patrol car went flying by.

"Hey! No ticket! What do you know!" Eli exclaimed.

He took Jill's hand and looked into her eyes.

"Eli, I would really like to kiss you. I just don't think that would be what Father wants us to do."

Eli asked, "You mean your dad?"

"No! I mean our heavenly Father," came Jill's sweet answer.

Thumbnail was dancing with glee. "I told you guys you needed me. You do the flashy stuff, but I get the job done."

Eli took Jill home.

Her dad was standing at the door. "Eli, I want to talk to you!"

"Yes, sir! What is it you would like to discuss with me?" Eli asked.

Jill went inside.

Mr. Thomas continued. "Eli, you are eighteen. You are a walking hormone. I just need to know what your intentions are toward my daughter," he said.

Eli's response was immediate. "Sir, my intentions are to honor God both on and off the ball field. I have not even kissed her yet."

"Yet?" came Jill's dad's immediate response.

"Mr. Thomas, I would be a liar if I told you I did not want to kiss Jill at some point, but Father has not allowed it," Eli responded.

"Eli, let me just say that a kiss has a lot of power in it. A kiss will open doors of passion that I don't think you two are ready for. This might sound like I am a stick in the mud, but if you wait to kiss a girl until you actually marry her, you might find that your relationship after marriage is much hotter than you ever thought it could be.

"You are serious?" Eli asked.

"Yes, Eli, I am serious," Jill's dad responded sternly.

Then Thumbnail whispered in Eli's ear, "Listen to him, Eli. The benefits are going to be out of this world."

Eli got real quiet and then responded. "Mr. Thomas, I think I have a lot to pray about. I have not even considered that position. Maybe I should," Eli said.

Then Father said, "Pete, you are about to see what being set apart really means."

"Mr. Thomas, let me get this straight. You think it is better if I do not kiss Jill until our wedding day?"

Smiling, Mr. Thomas responded. "You got it! You can hug her, you can hold her hand, but you can't kiss her, with the exception of a holy kiss on the forehead."

"Okay. You are the boss. I will go by your rules. This won't be easy," Eli said.

Jill came walking down the steps. "Eli, Dad has not beat you up too bad, has he?"

"Not at all. A piece of cake. But, hon, I do have an early day tomorrow. I think I will call it a night and try to get some sleep." As he walked away, he mumbled to himself, "Not." Eli got into the Challenger and hit the gas pedal hard. The tires screamed as he flew down the street.

"Guess something frustrated him, "Mr. Thomas offhandedly remarked before he could stop it.

"Daddy! What did you say to him?" Jill demanded.

"I just told him he could not kiss you until your wedding day!" her dad said coyly.

"You what? You told him what? Mom!" Jill screamed.

Eli flew up his street, roared into the driveway, and got out, slamming the car door.

Leah came running outside. "Eli, what's wrong?"

Again, Thumbnail whispered into Eli's ear, "Settle down. Just settle down. Her dad was right. It will be worth the wait."

Eli leaned against the Challenger. "You know what this car is named, right? This is going to be a challenge."

Back at Jill's house, Jill asked, "Mom, how can you let Dad be such an...*oh*!"

"Jill, just calm down," Jill's mom said soothingly. "I think your dad might be right, at least for a while. Have fun and see where God is going to take this. You are eighteen. Just trust us, and especially trust God in this."

Thumbnail was sitting on Eli's shoulder, whispering, "Eli, let's just keep this under control. She is a beautiful girl. Father has your life in His hands and hers as well. Trust Him! Have a good time, and do not do anything stupid," he said.

Eli asked himself, *Where are these thoughts coming from? They make so much sense. I better give Jill a call.*

"Jill, phone!" her mom said.

Jill ran across the living room and grabbed the phone from her mom.

"Hello!"

"Sweetie, this is going to come as a shock, but as much as I would love to kiss you, I think your dad might be right, at least for a while."

"You are serious?" Jill answered quickly.

"Yes. He did say I could give you hugs and I could hold your hand, just not kiss you except for a holy kiss on the forehead. I don't know what chemistry happens with that first kiss. I do want it to be with you, but I am willing to wait for God's timing, not mine."

"Pete, I think he's getting it. I knew he would come to that understanding. My time is their wedding day. As I have his career take off, kids are going to flock to him. The example he will be will blow people away," Father stated majestically.

Eli walked into the clubhouse. Phil Smith decided it is time to find out just what Eli is getting from Jill. So he asked. "Eli, I bet Jill's tight bottom feels pretty good, huh."

Eli grabbed Smith by the collar and rammed him against the locker. "If you ever, I mean ever, say something like that about Jill again, I am going to drive my fist so far down your throat that they are going to have to give you a rectal exam to find it."

Thumbnail jumped off Eli's shoulder. He did not even want to be close if this exploded.

Just then, Jim Ross jumped in between them. "Smith, knock it off. You just can't stomach anyone with a few morals, can you?"

The next day, they were on the bus early, heading to Beloit to play the Bombers. Eli was still madder than a wet hen.

"Pete, today, Eli finds out what being a professional is all about," Father said.

"What do you mean, Father?"

"Just watch, Pete!"

Eli stepped on the mound. He was not tossing the ball in the air. It was clear that something had really got him upset. He walked the first three batters and then gave up a homerun. Eli's manager stormed out to the mound and said, "McBrien, get your head on straight. What is going on with you today?"

Eli explained the whole thing with Smith.

"Eli, you are a professional now. You have to be able to put this crap out of your mind and do your job."

Eli nodded, tossed the ball in the air, and proceeded to strike out the rest of the lineup throughout the remainder of the game. However, it was to be Eli's only loss of the season. The grand slam did him in.

Arriving back in International Falls at midnight, to his surprise, Jill was waiting for Eli in the parking lot.

"Eli, what happened in the first inning?"

"I really don't want to talk about it," Eli responded.

"Eli, you need to be able to talk to me about anything."

"One of the guys on the team made a comment that really made me angry. It was about you. Once the coach came out to the mound and told me to settle down and I heard this soft little voice tell me that now I knew how much I really do care, I was able to concentrate on what I was doing. It was too late for that game, but it will never happen again," Eli responded.

"What did he say about me?"

"You really don't want to know."

"Yes, I do," Jill answered quickly.

"Okay. It had to do with your bottom. Can we just leave it at that?"

"We can."

"Good!"

The two hopped into the Challenger and drove the one hundred miles from International Falls to Roseau. As they were driving, Eli reached over and took Jill's hand.

"There is a rumor floating around that I might be getting called to Los Angeles."

"Eli, that would be great!"

"I know we are young," Eli replied.

"Eli, not yet. It is too early."

"I don't want to go without you," Eli answered.

"How about if I attend UCLA or maybe a Christian school out there," Jill offered.

As they pulled into the driveway, Eli got a little glint in his eye. "I need to talk to your dad." He walked her to the door and gave her a hug and a kiss on the forehead.

"Eli!" Jill said sternly.

"That, my dear, was a holy kiss," Eli said.

Jill's dad came to the door. "Mr. Thomas, I would like a word with you," Eli asked with the utmost respect.

"Sure, Eli. Come in. Jill, leave us alone please."

"Mr. Thomas, I don't want to go to Los Angeles without Jill. I want to marry Jill. There, I said it," Eli stated.

"Eli, if after her freshman year of college, you feel the same way, I will give you my blessing," came her dad's response.

"Pete, they have choices to make, many of them, but the key to their future is seeking my will. They are doing it right. I always work through structure and order. Eli is following that here," the Father said with total resolve.

"Father, when they get to Los Angeles, the parental involvement will diminish. How does your Word get through to them during those nights when they will be alone and hormones will be raging?" Pete asked.

"Pete, don't forget my secret weapon: Thumbnail," was the answer Father gave.

Secret Ambition

It was 5:30 a.m. on Monday, February 15, 2017. The phone was ringing, and the answering machine picked it up. The phone stopped ringing and started ringing again. Grace ran down and grabbed the phone.

"Is this Mrs. McBrien?"

"It is," replied Grace.

"This is Thomas Hill from Los Angeles. Is Eli in?"

Grace ran up the stairs. "Eli, Thomas Hill from the—" She did not have a chance to finish her sentence.

Eli was downstairs grabbing the phone. "Eli here."

"Eli, we are prepared to offer you three million dollars the first year, with a bonus for winning twenty games and all the usual stuff. We need you on the plane we are sending to the International Falls airport in two hours. Have your attorney there to look over the contract. You will want to get an agent for your next contract. If you have the success I think you will, the contract will be much bigger."

"Mr. Hill, give me a minute please." Eli set the phone down, walked across the room, and jumped in the air, throwing his arms up and yelling, "Yes!"

Eli returned to the phone and calmly said, "Mr. Hill, I will be at the airport in two hours with my attorney." With that, he hung up the phone.

Eli called his attorney. "Stan, this is Eli. Sorry to wake you up, but Los Angeles has a plane waiting for me. They want me to sign a contract before I fly out to LA in two hours. Can you meet me at the airport?"

"Eli, you know it. But I am charging you for this. How big is the contract?"

"Three million dollars!"

"We want a signing bonus of three hundred thousand. I will take fifty grand of it," Stan said.

"What?" Eli replied.

"Welcome to the world of big-time sports," was Stan's response.

"Pete, Eli is entering a world he knows nothing about. He has dreamed of this his whole life. Get Thumbnail. If he needs help, call out my biggest, meanest angels," Father said.

"Gotcha, Father," Pete answered.

Eli grabbed the phone. "Jill, I just got a call from Thomas Hill, LA's manager. They offered me three million dollars." Eli had to hold the phone away from his head because Jill was screaming so loudly. "I need to talk to your dad."

Jill asked, "About what? Eli, it is six in the morning."

"Just put your dad on the phone please," Eli said.

"Father, did I do right? You wanted me to whisper to Eli, for him to ask her dad if he can marry Jill, didn't you?" Thumbnail asked.

"Yes, Thumbnail. You did it exactly right," the Father responded.

"Mr. Thomas, I have just been offered a contract with Los Angeles."

"Eli, that is great! But why are you waking me up at six in the morning to tell me this?"

"Because I would love to be doing this in person, but I can't. I have to be on a plane in an hour and ten minutes, and I want to marry Jill!"

"Eli, I can see you are a man of honor. How about marrying Jill in June of next year? That will get you through the season. That is assuming Jill says yes," Jill's dad responded.

"Thumbnail, you whispered to Jill's dad as well?"

"I did, Father. Did I do well?"

"Yes, Thumbnail, you did well."

"Father, your praise is all I need. To hear you say, 'Well done,' boosts my spirit," Thumbnail responded.

Jill's dad handed Jill the phone. Jill asked, "Eli, what did you want to ask me?"

"Jill, I just asked your dad something, and he said yes."

"Eli, are you sure you want to do it, like this?"

"I am leaving today for LA. I will be getting a huge amount of money. The temptation that comes from it, I want to avoid it as much as possible. I love you too much to take that chance."

"Eli, let me meet you at the airport. Ask me there. That gives you an hour to pray about it."

"Pete, Thumbnail really did handle that well. I think we should increase his caseload," The Most High stated.

"Father, you are always right. I just follow orders."

"Pete, let's get these kids through this first year and married. Then we will give Thumbnail a much heavier caseload. I have just the person in mind," the Great I AM stated with a matter-of-fact manner that showed total authority.

In February, it was still dark at 7:00 am. Eli's mom brought him to the airport. Jill was already there. The guys from the head office were there to get a signature, so Eli had his attorney standing there. Stan grabs the contract and headed onto the plane where there was better light to read it.

Eli and Jill walked as far away from the crowd as they could get. "Jill, I have loved you since the first time I saw you. I have not had a chance to get you a ring. But will you marry me?"

Jill could hardly hold back the tears. Eli saw the little nod.

"Yes, I will marry you," Jill answered almost inaudibly.

"What was that? I could hardly hear you?"

"Yes, Eli McBrien, I will marry you!" Jill shouted.

All of a sudden, the lights of every car came on them. Stan ran up to Eli. "They will have a revised contract for you to sign in LA. They are giving you the three hundred-grand signing bonus. Now, get on the plane."

Eli gave Jill a long hug and then hopped on the plane. Three hours later, Eli was sleeping as they land at LAX. Eli got off the plane, and reporters were everywhere.

I am not going to like this, Eli thought to himself.

Eli walked down the tarmac as reporters screamed questions at him. He stopped, leaned into his new manager, and says, "Let me stop and have just a few words with them." Eli hopped up three steps of the jet's ladder. "Guys, gals, settle down and be a little quiet. I will make a statement."

The reporters got really quiet.

"I am going to make you a promise. Through my career, I know there will be positives and negatives. I will always be willing to take a second to talk to you. However, don't hound me. If you hound me, I will clam up. I have done nothing in the majors yet, so let me just get out of here and go to work," Eli said.

The reporters left.

"Father, that Thumbnail really knew what words to give Eli, didn't he?" Pete asked.

"Pete, that was all Eli."

"Wow. You have gotten him together," Pete said.

"Pete, when someone gives themselves to me, I give them a heart for all people. Eli knew they were only trying to do their job. He will give them what he can," the great I AM said.

Stan and Eli walked into the office of LA's owner, Michael Johnsmith. Mr. Johnsmith asked, "So, Eli, you want a three hundred-thousand-dollar signing bonus? Here is what we are going to do. You play this year on your one-year contract. Next year, if you win me twenty games, we will sign a contract that will be so big you will not have any money worries for the rest of your life. If you win me thirty games, your contract will be even bigger."

Eli looked at Stan, knowing he wouldn't like it.

"Mr. Johnsmith, how about a little incentive for this kid. Let's say for every game over twenty that he wins, he gets an extra hundred thousand dollars?"

"Now that is an interesting offer. Sarah, that contract you have sitting on your computer, add into it any game over twenty that Eli wins, he gets an extra hundred grand. I like incentives!" Johnsmith answered.

"Before I sign this, I need to ask if you will fly us back to Roseau in your jet. I need to see Jill for a few moments before I head to Florida for spring training."

A few minutes later, Sarah brought the new contract in and handed it to Eli, who promptly gave it to Stan.

Stan said, "Yes, this is a good contract. Eli, go ahead and sign it." Eli signed it.

Mr. Johnsmith said, "Eli, here is a check, minus taxes, of course, that should get you through the next couple of weeks."

"Mr. Johnsmith, this check is for a hundred and fifty thousand dollars," Eli stated with amazement.

"Eli, you are going to have moving expenses, and word has it you have an engagement ring to buy."

Eli walked out of the office and went down the street to the nearest bank. He walked in, and the bank president walked up to Eli.

"Mr. McBrien, may I help you?"

"I need to set up an account today and have a cash card in my hand before I leave this bank," Eli said.

In twenty-five minutes, they had a cash card in Eli's hand and had cashed his check.

Eli's next stop was Tiffany's. He picked out a very expensive ring. Then he walked out, hopped in the limo that was waiting for him, and went back to the private jet. As soon as he was in the air, Eli grabbed his phone.

"Jill, hi. We are landing in International Falls in about two hours on our way to Florida for spring training. I have something for you. We should be there in about two hours." Eli said.

As soon as they had landed in International falls, Eli walked off the plane. Jill ran up to Eli and threw her arms around him. Eli dropped to one knee and pulled out the ring. (The diamond was so large that it almost glowed in the dark.)

"I am going to do this right this time. Jill, will you marry me?"

Jill started to hyperventilate. "Yes!"

"Jill, take a breath," Eli said.

"Father, they are a bit young, are they not?" Pete stated.

"Not at all. I do things for their protection. Eli is going to have hundreds of girls going gaga over him. He will have offers to model clothes that Thumbnail will whisper in his ear to turn down. Remember, I do have everything under control," Father stated in a matter-of-fact voice.

"But, Father, where does his freedom of choice come in?" Pete asked.

"He always has the choice not to follow me. Eli knows where his strength comes from. He knows the woman I have put in front of him loves him and I. He might slip up, but he will never leave," the great I AM answered.

Eli looked at Jill and said, "Babes, you have to know that I would love to stay and celebrate. But I have to get back on this plane to get to Florida for spring training and earn some of this money that I am spending." With that and a quick hug, Eli jumped back on the plane.

Eli got off the plane in Orlando, hopped in the car waiting for him, and headed out to LA's training facilities. He arrived at two in the morning, dropped off his equipment, and went to his hotel. As he lay in bed, his mind was going over the day's activities. He prayed, "Father, what are you doing with me? This whole baseball thing, how are you going to use me?"

Thumbnail, sitting on his bedpost, whispered to Eli, "Eli, your greatness is going to touch hundreds of young boys and girls. Father has destined you for this from the beginning of time. Hang on. The ride is going to be great!"

Eli looked around the room and thought to himself, *Who said that?* Eli shrugged his shoulders and shut the lights off and went to sleep.

It was four thirty in the morning. The banging on his door woke him. Eli demanded, "What is going on?"

"McBrien, get your butt out of bed. This is the real world. Move it!"

Eli jumped up, threw his clothes on, got on the bus, and headed for the ballpark. When Eli arrived, he heard the pitching coach yelling, "Pitchers, see those steps? I want you to run over every step in this stadium. I want it flat out. Be back here in twenty minutes. Go!"

Eli started running. For the first few flights, he had no problems. But as the seconds turned into minutes, his thighs started to burn. He kept up the full-tilt run. He kept working, finally reaching the top of the last set of steps, and headed back down to the field. He ran up to the coach, who promptly told Eli to hit the weight room.

Eli worked the weights with the same intensity that he did back in elementary school, when Father first put

His spirit in him to build within him the motivation that would get him through the rest of his life. It also would turned him into the baseball-pitching machine that no one could hit.

His teammates were in total awe with his ability to lift weights and the speed he was able to increase them.

Len Johnston, the first baseman, was the most surprised. He asked, "Eli, you are such a little guy. Your muscles should be bigger than Brad's over there. How do you do it?"

"I have some good friends in high places," Eli answered.

"You must. I never have seen a little guy throw weights around like you do," Len responded.

"Sometime, I will share the whole story with you. Right now, we have a season to get ready for," was his intense answer.

"You rookies go gung ho on everything," Len said to Eli.

"Look, Len. We are being paid a lot of money to play a kid's game. I would think you would want to feel like you are earning it from day one," Eli responded.

The look on Len's face could freeze a popsicle in a second. He turned and walked away.

Eli got back to lifting weights with Thumbnail on his shoulder, who was saying, "Go, Eli. Go Eli. Go Eli!" over and over.

Eli thought it was his own thoughts, *Why would I think thoughts like that?* Eli questioned himself. He continued thinking, *It is almost as if there is a coach inside of me.*

Eli worked hard for the first three weeks. The rest of the team caught his spirit, with Thumbnail bouncing from player to player, urging them on.

It came time for their first game in the Grapefruit League. When they sent Eli to the mound, the manager told Eli, "Let them hit you. Make them ask, 'Where did they get this buffoon?'"

"Why?" Eli asked.

"Eli, these games mean nothing to us. We don't want to give anything away in them."

Eli went out and let them hit him out of the park. He got pulled after the second inning. Los Angeles lost 15 to 1. In the locker room, Eli was really upset. He said, "I felt like a girl pitching today."

Eli's manager said, "Look, Eli, you really don't want these guys trying to figure out how to hit you. I have been in this league long enough to understand that someone is going to figure out how to hit you. You just don't want it to happen to soon. "

April 1, 2017, was the season opener for Los Angeles. The excitement was totally crazy. The stadium was full, and Eli was starting. He had flown his mom and brothers and sisters out to the game. Jill was already out there and was sitting in the box with Eli's mom. Eli was in the locker room, throwing up. He had just looked out at the field and saw the thousands upon thousands of fans waiting for him to strike out his first batter.

"It's time to go," announced his manager.

The team walked up the runway. Eli ran out with the team. He looked up to where Grace and Jill and the rest of them were and waved at them as he walked out on the field. Eli threw a few balls to warm up as he got ready for the first batter.

The national anthem played. Michelle Goldsmith was singing it.

Helen Johnson, the first woman president, threw out the first pitch.

After her successful pitch, Eli shook hands with her, smiled, and got ready to get down to business. As he was standing there, he was thinking back to his Little League days, to the first time he took the mound with the pain in his hips. And here he was now. Then Eli's mind returned to his high school years, the youth group, and Michael W. Smith's "Secret Ambition." He heard the pounding instrumentals, knowing his secret ambition was not just to be the greatest pitcher ever but to see millions of kids come to Christ through his baseball. He felt the music. He imagined himself in front of the youth group. He heard the drums, felt his guitar, looked at the ball in his hand, and then looked to heaven, made the sign of the cross, and tossed the ball up in the air.

Eli looked down at his catcher, Matt Smith, for the signal, which was a fastball at the knees. Eli put the ball at the knees straight across. The gun said 98 miles per hour. The batter did not even get his bat off his shoulder. Next, he threw another fastball. This time it was 102 miles per hour.

Roger Bacus, doing color commentary, asked, "How fast can this kid throw?"

The next ball Eli put in at 105 miles per hour, and the batter went down without even swinging his bat.

"Pete, I did it, and I get the credit! Watch what he does to this next batter. It is going to be so cool."

Eli looked down at John San Deigo, the next batter. He tossed the ball and then winked. The batter went nuts. Eli looked at him, shook his head, and looked almost like he pitied the guy. He tossed the ball again, looked into Matt's space, and got the signal for a fastball. Eli decides to go with maximum velocity, and it hits Matt's glove at 108. Matt jumped up and took his glove off. His hand is in extreme pain from the momentum of the pitch. Matt signaled for a curve. Eli waved it off and instead threw another fastball. Again, the same results occurred. Strike two. Matt signaled for a changeup. Eli smiled and looked up at his mom. She saw him wink. She knew what was coming, the changeup she taught him. Eli wound up. The ball looked like it's another fastball until it got to the plate. Then it dropped like a rock and the batter was out.

The rest of the game continued the same way, and Eli got his first shutout in the major leagues. As he walked off the field, his teammates stormed him.

Eli said, "Hey, guys, there are only a hundred and sixty-one games left. We need to keep our eyes on the prize," Eli said.

"What's the prize, the Series?" one of the teammates asked Eli.

"No. The prize is Christ and his kingdom. The rest will follow as a result of the prize."

"See. I told you, Pete. He will give me the glory."

"Father, you are always right," Peter responded.

Grace and Jill were waiting for Eli at the locker room door. "Mom, I think tomorrow I need to hunt for an apartment," Eli said.

"Eli, I think that is a great idea. Can I help?" Jill's sweet voice asked.

"Babes, of course, you can help. As a matter of fact, why don't you pick it out? I trust you."

The next day, Grace and Jill went looking for apartments for Eli. Grace, being the mom that she was, started looking for apartments in her income range. "Grace, why are we looking at apartments in this neighborhood? Eli can afford any apartment he wants," Jill asked.

"Where should we look?" Grace asked Jill.

"Brentwood," answered Jill quickly. "Look at this one three bedrooms, a sauna, a Jacuzzi, stone floor in the bathroom, six thousand a month."

"Let's look at it," Grace replied as they got in the car that the team provided for them and headed to the address they had found in Brentwood.

During practice on Tuesday, the manager came up to Eli and said, "Eli, we have to start working on more defensive moves for you during the game. You have not had to work in a situation where you have guys on base, and you have to try to figure out how to get them out."

"No one can hit me. No one has ever been able to hit me. But you pay me big money, so I will do anything you ask," Eli answered.

"I want Kip Johnson to be on first. He is going to try to steal second. Eli, your job is to deliver the ball as quickly as you can to Matt. Matt throws to Simpson on second, and Kip should be out."

Smith was the batter. Kip took a lead. Eli looked at Kip, heard the music, and realized right now his secret ambition is to get Kip out. Eli sets. Kip took his lead, and then Eli, with a quick throw, almost without turning, flipped the ball over in a way that Kip could not see it until it was too late. He was out.

The team continued the move several times until they had it down.

Their next game was against Frisco. Fred Lemue, the center fielder for the Bridges, had been studying Eli's last game. He was trying to figure out how to hit him. He had never seen a fastball quite that fast but knew that there had to be a way of beating Eli. Hour after hour, he watched him pitch. Fred watched Eli's feet before each pitch, watching his stance, trying to figure out where the pitch was going before he threw it. He slows the pitch down. The fastball was at the same spot each time he threw it.

I've got him! Fred thought to himself.

The alarm sounded. It was 5:30 a.m. Eli jumped in the shower, ran down to the lobby, hopped in the car that was waiting for him, and headed for the field. He got to his locker, dressed in his uniform, and walked out into the empty stadium. He was not starting today but was being held in relief. Tom Henderson, the team manager, wanted to hold him in that position. He thought if he had him throw relief, he could make that rocket last longer. The plan was to start him three games a month and hold him in relief the rest of the time. Eli did not like it, but he was told that that is the way it is going to be.

"Father, Eli is getting a huge lesson in humility," Peter said.

"Peter, you are absolutely right there. The pros have many games a year. The manager's job is to get the best performance out of every member of his team, much like the ideal situation for a pastor. His job is to lead the flock where I tell him they need to go. He has to be able to relate to each person what part of my purpose they have. Encourage them to be the best they can be, making full use of all the talents that I have given them," Father responded.

It was game day. Los Angeles was facing San Francisco. Through the first eight innings, Eli sat on the bench. Los Angeles was leading by a run, and all of a sudden, Eli got the call to warm up. Eli grabbed his glove and headed to the warm-up mound. He started throwing slowly, feeling the muscles loosen. Every pitch had a little more on it. He started throwing at seventy-four miles per hour. He nodded that the warm-up felt great. At the top of the ninth, Eli was sent out to pitch. Fred Lemue was up to bat. He looked at Eli, smiled, and sent the message, "I have you all figured out."

There was one little problem with this one. Thumbnail knew this guy had something on Eli. He whispered to Eli, "No fastballs with this guy. Throw him two curves, one inside, one outside, and then a changeup. But use your fastball stance."

Eli looked around and thought to himself, *Who said that?*

Matt signaled for a fastball. Eli shook his head. The signal came for a curve inside. Yes, that's the one. Eli threw the curve from a fastball stance. Strike one. The next pitch was a curveball inside.

Lemue shook his head and thought to himself, *Where is the fastball?*

Eli looked down. Lemue looked at Eli. He figured from the stance. This was it. He was getting ready for a fastball. Eli wound up, and the ball floated. Lemue swung a half second early. Eli smiled and got ready for the next batter.

Stan Johnston came to the plate. Matt signaled for a fastball. Eli gave him one at a 100 miles per hour. Stan swung and missed, but his timing on it was perfect. Eli looked at Matt. He saw the same thing and a call for maximum speed. Eli threw the next pitch at 108. Stan could not even get the bat around. Next, Matt signaled for a slider. This was a pitch that Eli had been working on for the last couple of weeks. Eli nodded. Stan swung and was out.

The next batter was Peter Reed. He was a rookie who was really out to make a name for himself. But he wouldn't off Eli. The call was for a curve low and inside. Eli threw it. Peter got a piece of it and drove it deep. It was an easy catch for right fielder Sam Bursa. The side was retired.

The game was over, and both teams walked off the field.

Sam Bursa came up to Eli after the game and asked, "What do you have? What in the world makes you be able to pitch that well? Your natural talent blows me away. When Reed got a hold of that ball, it woke me up. You are really a boring pitcher to play with. When we are in the outfield, man, there is no action."

"Look, Sam. It's not me. It's really not. There is this little voice I hear."

"That's me. It really, really is," Thumbnail let out.

"C'mon, Eli. There is more to that. There has to be. I have seen you work out. You are a man possessed."

"Well, maybe I am possessed, but it's by the Holy Spirit of God himself!"

Sam said, "We play Seattle next. Do you pitch?"

Eli answered, "I don't think I will start. I might go in as a relief pitcher."

"Father, it is June. They have a bunch of games left. How does he keep the intensity that he needs to be able to handle what you are putting in front of him to do?" Pete asked.

"Jill will keep his spirits up. She is going to be his biggest cheerleader. Don't worry about Eli," Father answered.

Eli and Sam were walking out of the stadium, and Jill was trying to get close to the player's gate so she could meet Eli when he came out.

Hank, the guard, was standing there. "Excuse me, little girl. Where do you think you are going?"

Jill answered, "I am going to meet my fiancé!"

"Who might that be?" came the gruff response.

"Eli McBrien," she anwered sweetly.

"I don't think so," Hank said sarcastically. "You little hotties will say anything to get close to those guys." Hank had no idea who he was dealing with.

Jill lifted her hand and said, "Mister, see this ring?"

"Miss, these players make so much money they can buy those by the—"

"Sweetheart, is there a problem?" Eli asked as he walked up behind Jill.

"Eli, this man called me a hottie and told me that I am not allowed into the player's area. He said the ring meant nothing to him," Jill said, almost crying.

Eli asked, "Hank, is that true?"

"Yes, Mr. McBrien. Pretty much," Hank answered.

"How long have you worked here?"

"About ten years."

"Well, Hank, this is my fiancée. She is the love of my life. You will never see anyone else coming here claiming to know me. If you do, they are lying. If she wants to come in, you let her. Is that understood?"

"Yes, Mr. McBrien. It is clear."

Just then, Sam came up with his wife, Corrin.

"Pete, watch this. I am about to use Eli and Jill, and Sam and Corrin to break down walls. These kids hear My voice. They want to be used by Me. I will use them to touch hearts of the kids they come in contact with. Just watch as I create something really beautiful," Father said.

Sam said to Eli, "Eli, I help run our church youth group. I could surely use your help with that bunch of kids."

"Sam, I can't give you an answer to that right now. I have a lot on my plate. But if that's where Father is leading, that's what I will do. I know that the kids have to be touched, but I am not going to commit to something that I cannot follow through on."

"Tell you what, Eli, we are off on Sunday. What do you say we go to church together and then out to lunch afterward?"

Jill said, "We'd love to."

"Wait a minute, Jill. Where does what I want come in?"

"Eli, sweetie, why would you not want to worship with me on Sunday morning?" Jill asked with a sly grin on her face.

"Guess we'll see you in church on Sunday," Eli answered wisely. "Jill, then I presume you are willing to go with me to mass on Saturday?"

"Of course I would Eli," Jill answered sweetly.

"Father, I thought you said Eli would become part of what Sam is doing?" Pete asked.

"Pete, how many times have you seen the idea planted and it takes time for it to come to fruition? The plan I have planted is much more complex than one youth group in one little church. I know what I am doing. Trust me," Father responded.

The rest of the season was kind of a blur. The pitching staff would get the team in a jam, and Eli would have to try and get them out game after game. They would not start Eli. They had bigger plans for the 2018 season next year.

At the end of the season, Eli had a fat bank account and Jill was busy planning a wedding. Jill called Eli from her mom's house and asked him how much she could spend.

Eli, in his usual manner, said, "I don't know. Let me come over and give you my cash card." Eli got in the Challenger and drove the few miles to Jill's. He walked to the door and knocked. Jill came to the door and gave Eli a huge hug. They walked inside, holding hands. Eli pulled out his wallet. "Babe, here is the cash card. I think there is one point five million in it. Spend two hundred and fifty thousand dollars. That should be good."

Jill's jaw dropped. "How much?"

Eli repeated, "Two hundred and fifty thousand max, not a penny more. Is that understood?"

Jill's mom called Grace. "Are we going to let them spend that kind of money on their wedding?"

Grace answered, "It is their money."

A short time later, Eli's agent called him. "Eli, I think we have an offer on the table that's worth taking a serious look at. They are offering fifty million dollars over five years! What do you think?"

Eli quickly said, "Tell them to get the contract ready. We will sign it today!"

Bible Baseball

Eli walked out of mass on Saturday night. The priest stopped him and asked, "Mr. McBrien, would you be willing to help with the young people in our church?"

"You mean like a youth group?" Eli asked.

"That's exactly what I meant, Mr. McBrien."

"First, it's Eli. Tell you what. I have a buddy who is the youth director at his church. You know, at First Church, over on Fifth Avenue. Let's combine the youth groups."

"Eli, I don't want anyone trying to talk these kids out of being good Catholics."

"Father, our concern is that these kids grow in Christ. We are going to work towards that goal. When we get done with them, they will be better Lutherans, Catholics, or whatever they want to be. But they will have a commitment to Christ first." Eli said.

"I reserve the right to pull the plug anytime," the priest said.

Eli responded, "Let me remind you who asked who to do this. I either get free reign or—"

"Okay. I guess it is my turn to trust," the priest answered.

Eli arrived home. Jill had been in church with her parents back in Roseau. Eli was all excited and called her. "How are the plans for the wedding coming, babes?"

Jill answered, "They are coming along really great."

Eli excitedly shared, "The priest asked me to take on the youth group in the off-season. I have to talk to Sam about this, but I wanted to combine it with the one he does at his church."

Jill responded with, "You know, Eli, June first is coming super quickly. I need some of your input into this wedding. I don't want to do this all on my own."

"Okay. Tell me what kind of input you want from me. Do you want help with picking tablecloths, colors, or silver? Babes, do you really want me involved with this, or do you just want me closer to you?" Eli asked Jill.

Jill answered, "To be honest, I just want you close to me."

"Jill you sounded a bit panicked. You seem to be totally overwhelmed by this whole thing. So here is what I want you to do. Is your Bible close? Eli asked.

"It's right here," Jill responded.

"Open it to Philippians 4:7 and read it to me," Eli said.

"And the peace of God which passes all understanding will keep your heart and mind in Christ Jesus," Jill read. "Eli, I see it; I understand it. But I still want you close," Jill pleaded.

"Jill, I have a question for you. Did you hear a word I said when I first called?" Eli asked the best gift Father had given him.

"To be honest, no," came the truthful answer from Jill.

"Okay, let me restate what my priest asked me. He wants me to run the youth group for him at the church."

Jill said, "Eli, that's great, but I still would love to have you close to me while I work on the wedding."

"That's what I thought," Eli replied. Eli continued, "Here's my idea. I will talk to Sam to see what he thinks of the idea of the combined youth group. Then, if he likes the idea, we can do the planning for the youth groups over the phone. I will fly out one day a week for the combined youth group."

"Eli, Father has really put these kids on your heart, hasn't he?" Jill asked.

"Yes, He really has. You come first. You always will. A lot of these kids have nothing. The parents might have all the money in the world but they have no foundation in their lives. They don't understand what love really is. If I can help them, I will."

Jill replied, "Eli, I have an idea. You go and call Sam I have to take care of something on this end. Call me back in five minutes, would you?"

With that Eli called Sam.

Sam answered his cell. "Eli what's going on?" Sam asked.

"Sam, I was walking out of church yesterday, and the priest asked me to run his youth group. I suggested we combine yours with ours. It would be a great way for the two of us to work together and see if we could be Father's instruments in getting all of these kids turned on to Christ and his kingdom," Eli answered.

Sam responded instantly, "Eli, that's a great idea. I think we need to get the girls involved with this."

"Let's do it," Eli responded. Then a light went on inside his head. "Bible baseball," Eli said.

"Bible baseball?" Sam answered in a questioning tone.

"Yeah! It would be a great icebreaker. The kids learn the Word and have a little competition. We get both churches to root for their team. What do you think, buddy?" Eli answered.

"Let's do it," came Sam's quick response

Eli then called Jill back. He got the surprise of his life when she answered the phone.

"Hi, sweetheart," Eli said.

"Eli, can you fly me out there? I have just gotten off the phone with Corrin Bursa. If you get me a ticket, I can be out there tonight and spend the night with them. That way, the four of us can lay out this plan for how we are going to reach these kids."

"Jill, great idea! That way you could work with Corrin on how the girls' needs could be met. We have also come up with an icebreaker that will get these kids working together. I have one that might work."

"What's that, sweetheart?" asked Jill sweetly.

"Bible baseball," Eli answered.

"Bible baseball! Eli that should be interesting. How is it gonna work?" asked the one God had chosen for Eli.

"We take a couple of weeks and sit down with our kids. We have them dig through the Bible to find scriptures and then write questions about it. Then we get together with the other group and have a competition. Easy questions that are answered correctly are singles. Harder and harder ones would be doubles, triples, and homeruns. Homeruns are going to be scriptures that the respective church doctrines have been built on. When they answer them, they have to be done in a non-judgmental way that showed an understanding of the doctrine as well as the scripture that backed it. What we are trying to do here is build unity in diversity," Eli said.

"Eli that is a wonderful goal! Can you carry it out?" Jill asked.

"Jill, I really think we can. If we couldn't, Father would not have placed us here to accomplish it," Eli answered.

Two weeks later, the phone rang.

"Eli here!"

"Eli, Sam here. How are you?"

"Sam, I am doing well. How are your guys doing as far as getting ready for the game next week?" Eli asked.

"Sam, buddy, before we talk Bible baseball, I have a question I have been wanting to ask you. In my senior year of high school I was used to help a young lad by the name of Aaron Bursa."

Before Eli could finish his thought, the answer came from Sam. "My cousin. I heard all about it."

Eli replied, "Hardest-working kid I ever saw. Anyway, now back to the Bible baseball again. You guys gonna be ready next week?"

"Don't worry about us. You guys better be ready. We are gonna kick your butts!" Sam's quick comeback caught Eli off guard.

"Sam, you really think you can touch us? Man, you do have something to learn," Eli replied.

The week passed quickly. Eli and Sam both pushed their kids to get them ready for the big showdown at the church.

As he pulled into the lot, Eli looked around and saw the parking lot filled with cars. "Oh no. I have not seen this many cars in the lot ever. I wonder what's going on?"

Eli walked inside. Catholics were on one side, and the Assembly church was on the other side. "What's going on?" Eli asked Sam.

"Oh, we thought a little fan backup on both sides would help. So I called your priest and my pastor and told them to pass the word that this was going on tonight," Sam answered.

The stage in the fellowship hall was decorated in baseball regalia, nine chairs on each side of the stage and a baseball diamond in the middle.

Eli asked himself, *How did I get myself into this?* Eli looked at Jill. She was smiling from ear to ear. Eli asked her, "Babes, what are you smiling about?"

"Eli, don't you realize how great this is? You have the support of all the parents with this thing."

"Yeah. the problem is, I hope this goes as planned," Eli said.

Eli walked out to the middle of the stage. "Folks, I want to take this opportunity to thank you all for coming tonight. Both of the youth groups have been working really hard getting ready for this game tonight. Here's how it's going to work. Each team will have three outs in an inning. Both teams have spent time researching the Bible to find passages that they can use in the competition. There will be nine innings or two hours, whichever comes first. The team up to bat will choose the category of question that is asked them. Singles are the easiest, and then doubles, and then triples. For a homerun, it becomes a point of doctrine. The question is asked by the group holding to that doctrine. It has to be answered using the scripture that points to that doctrine. They are not allowed to give their view on whether that point of doctrine is correct or not; just the scripture reference that it points to. The purpose of this exercise is to help them understand the doctrines that divide and those that are very close. The goal is for understanding and to unite them in Christ. With that said, play ball!"

Eli's team was up to bat first. Their youngest player, Mike Howard, was up to bat. Mike, a nine-year-old, stated with confidence, "I would like a single."

Seth Saylor had the question for him. "What is the shortest verse in the Bible?"

Mike stated with excitement, "Jesus wept. John eleven thirty-five."

"That's right," Seth answered.

Shane Smith came up next. "I would like another single."

The question put to him by the opposing team was, "What is the second shortest verse in the Bible?"

All of a sudden, an extremely puzzled look came across Shane's face. "I don't know," he answered sheepishly.

The rules stated you had to be able to answer that question to get him out.

Seth then stated with total confidence, "It is, 'Eber, Peleg, Reu,' First Chronicles one twenty-five."

Sam popped open his laptop and confirmed the answer. "That is correct. Shane, you are out."

The questions went back and forth, back and forth. With ten minutes left to play, the churches were separated by only one run. The Assembly church was behind.

Sam took his team aside. "There is only one way we can win. We have to have a homerun. Jack, I want you up. You have to go for the homerun."

Eli then called the next person up.

Jack walked up to the microphone." I will take a homerun."

Ted Smith, from the Catholic church, took his microphone, looked over at Eli, and asked, "Mr. McBrien, the question I get to pose is on our doctrine, not theirs, correct?"

"Yes, that's correct," Eli answered.

"Jack, what is the doctrine of the Virgin Mary, and what scripture does the Catholic church use to support it?" he asked.

Jack responded, "This doctrine comes from Matthew one verses eighteen through twenty-five. It states that Mary was a virgin both at the conception and birth of Christ. Another interesting fact is the Muslims also believe Mary was a virgin at the birth of Christ. It is also pulled from Luke one: twenty-six through fifty-six and two: one through seven. The doctrine of the virgin birth is shared by all Christians. However, Matthew thirteen fifty-five and fifty-six casts doubt on her perpetual virginity." With that, Jack sat down.

Sam and Eli stepped aside to confer on the answer. They also pull up the Internet quickly to check out Jack's research. Eli's priest and Sam's pastor could be seen discussing the answer as well. All were wishing the question had not have been asked.

Eli looked at Sam.

Sam said, "If he had not thrown in that last verse, pointing out the question on the perpetual virginity, it would have been a homerun."

"But, Sam, he showed a command of the topic and that he had done his research first. He was prepared," Eli stated.

The look on Sam's face showed this was the hardest call he had ever had to make. "Eli, this would cost us the game. But this is what I would suggest. We call it a triple and we point out that the last scripture was used in a way that could cause division among the youth groups, hence, not a homerun."

Eli said, "I don't think we can do that. I think we have to give it a homerun. The reason is that he spoke the truth."

"Eli, truth is fine. But the point we made at the beginning was that we are doing this for an understanding of doctrines and where each church was coming from and not trying to refute the other's doctrine. How about if we ask Jack what his motives were in bringing up that counterpoint to the doctrine of Mary? Eli, the counterpoint is a valid point and might make points in a formal debate. This is not a debate. It is a game about Scripture. We are not asking for points that refute the doctrines of the other. They can do that on their own. What we are doing here is building understanding. Let's ask Jack what his motive was in the last part of his answer. I think I know, but let's ask him."

Sam looked over at Jack. "Jack, would you come over here please?"

Jack looked concerned as he walked over. "What do you need?"

Sam asked, "What was your motive in the last part of the question?"

Jack replied, "I wanted to show my Catholic friends that their belief of Mary being a virgin all her life was not true."

"Thank you. That's all we needed to know. You may take your seat."

Sam and Eli look at each other and in unison said, "Triple."

Eli walked up to the podium. "The last question resulted in a triple, giving the Catholics the win."

Jack stood up and said angrily, "I got that question right! That should have been a homerun!"

Sam took Jack aside. "You did not play by the rules. You were trying to cause conflict with that answer. We are trying to build unity here. There are differences. Those differences will never be agreed on. Conflict is not a way to win them over. There might be a time to approach differences. Tonight was not the time."

"Father, do you understand what happened here?" Peter asked.

"Pete, you are asking me if I understand? You are asking the Creator of the universe if I understand something?"

"Guess I missed on that one," Pete answered sheepishly.

"Here is what happened. Jack was trying to do a good thing, so his motives were correct. However, he did it by breaking the rules. Rules are meant to protect all involved. I let him go forward to teach him a lesson."

The next day, Sam gave Eli a call on his cell phone. "Eli, we are going on a hayride tomorrow. Care to get your kids and join us?"

"Let me call Jill and see what she says," Eli answered. Then Eli added, "I have a better idea. Why don't we fly them to Roseau? I have a farmer there, and we will take them on a horse-driven ride."

"That sounds great, Eli. How are all these kids going to pay for it?"

"Sam, let me ask you a question. How much money did you make last year?"

"Eli, I made a lot more than you did. What's the point?"

"It's simple, my friend. I will buy my kids their tickets and you buy yours."

"Man, Eli. Okay." And the agreement was reached.

Both men called their clergy to get their permission. The parents were called, and the permission slips were signed.

Eli and Sam figured out it was actually less expensive for them to rent a private jet and have the kids flown out to International falls. The problem they ran into was they had to get government permission to land the plane at an air force base, as there were no commercial airports nearby.

Eli called Los Angeles's owner and told him what he had in mind. The owner said, "Here's what I am going to do. Have your kids at LAX tomorrow at ten a.m. I will put them on my plane and fly them out. I will contact Feinstein and tell her what we need. I am sure she will cut some red tape for me. I gave her a lot of money for her last campaign."

The next day, Eli called his mom. "Mom, I have a surprise for you. I will be coming home this weekend and bringing a few friends."

Eli's mom asked, "How many?"

Eli answered, "Well, let's say eighty. There will be forty from my youth group and, say, another forty from the Assembly's youth group."

"What! Where? How?" Eli's mom asked.

"Mom, relax. You have three hours. We just took off."

"Where are your kids going to stay?" Eli's mom asked.

Eli responded, "On your floor."

"What? Eli, you are bringing eighty kids and giving me three hours' warning? How could you do that to me?"

"Mom, I would have given you more warning, but we decided an hour ago. We had to get a senator involved to get clearance to land at the air force base. Then we needed military buses to bring all of us to your house."

Grace looked at her house. It's pretty neat. But eighty kids plus her own here? She smiled to herself. Her mind went back to when Eli was a child, when he struggled just to learn to read. She thought about how impulsive he was at a young age. Grace chuckled to herself and thought, *He hasn't changed a bit.*

"Pete," Father mused, "when I created Moms, I did created miracle workers, did I not?"

"Yes, Father. They can take nothing and turn it into something. Can I speak freely?" Peter asked.

"Yes, Peter, speak freely."

"How is Grace going to do it with eighty kids and only three hours' notice?"

Father answered, "Watch me work."

At 3:00 p.m. central time, the Learjet with eighty people on it landed at the air force base in International Falls, Minnesota. The kids from both youth groups were bouncing off the ceiling.

Eli grabbed his cell phone and said, "Mom, we have decided that we are going to go out to the farm first. We should be there a couple of hours. We won't be eating breakfast tomorrow at your house. On the flight over, I made some calls. We are going to take the kids over to the restaurant in town for breakfast. The only thing we will need is sleeping space on your floor."

Grace sighed then smiled and said to herself, "There is something special about that boy. He loves kids. Someday he will be a great husband and father."

Arriving at the farm, Bill Jones, the owner of the farm, came out. Everyone saw the wagons as they came out of his barns with two teams of Clydesdales that came out to pull the wagons. The girls went nuts! Oohs and ahs came from all of them. They just about jumped on each other to get close enough to pet them.

Jayne Smith had an apple in her pocket that she brought along for a snack. She smiled, looked at Bill, and asked, "May I feed this to your horse?"

"Jayne, his name is Puffball. Go ahead."

Jayne tentatively walked up to Puffball. The horse turned his big head and saw Jayne holding the apple out. Being a gentle beast, the horse walked over and took the apple out of her hand without touching her hand.

For two hours, the kids sang Christmas songs as the horses pulled them on the wagons, taking them through rows and rows of pine trees. Eli put his arm around Jill. She put her head on his shoulder. Eli kissed the top of her head. She sighed. Eli saw the lights on the trees making her eyes glisten in the dark. Her smile brightened the furious life that he has had since he started his career with Los Angeles. They continually looked into each other's eyes. One could see the desire building within them that would be played out on their wedding night.

Soon, the ride ended. The kids went over to the fire, where they roasted hot dogs and marshmallows and drank hot chocolate. Everyone had a lot of fun and thanked Bill for the wonderful time. Then, sadly, it was time to get on the bus and head back to Grace's house. The kids were tired. They dragged their sleeping bags into the house. The living room, basement, and the hallways were filled with kids in sleeping bags on the floor.

Eli crawled out of his sleeping bag on the floor, early in the morning, and quietly snuck into the kitchen to have a cup of coffee with his mom. "Mom, I have worked it out with the Los Angeles staff for the wedding in June. I will pitch on the seventeenth. They will take me out of the rotation until the twenty-third. They say it's the best they can do. I pitch on the twenty-fourth against San Francisco."

The month of January passed quickly. Eli and Jill made plans for the wedding and flew back and forth to Los Angeles to work with the kids. February 15 came up quickly, which was the start of spring training in Florida.

A Father-Son Moment

Eli had begun his second full season. Having a fat new contract under his belt, Eli was ready to get going. For the last three weeks since the hayride, he had been like a caged lion. He would go to the gym and lift, run, and jump rope. He would do anything to burn energy. In the evening, he would be watching films or spending time with Jill. At times, he would do both at the same time.

"Eli, you are obsessed. How can you be so devoted to throwing a baseball faster and harder than anyone else in the world?" Jill asked.

"Hon, it's like this. Los Angeles is paying me a lot of money. I have to produce, and I will. The team heads for Ft. Lauderdale next week. So I will be gone for about four weeks."

"Eli, I'll sure miss you," Jill said as a tear ran down her cheek.

Eli put his arm around her and drew her to himself.

"Eli, can we go for a walk?"

"Sure, babes." They walked off her dad's porch.

"Eli, I want more physical contact with you. I want you to kiss me, touch me, and…"

"Pete, I knew this was coming, and I know what his answer is going to be," Father said calmly.

"What is he going to do, Father?" Peter asked.

"Just watch," was what the Father said.

"Jill, I made a promise to your dad. I won't go back on my word," Eli said.

"Eli, I really feel like I can trust you. That feels so safe and comforting. I just can't put it into words," Jill cooed.

"Jill, I only broke my word once. It hurt a lot of people. I will never let that happen again. There is nothing more important than keeping one's word. Nothing," Eli stated with intensity in his voice.

Eli hugged Jill. "I have to leave now. It's my job. Lots of people are depending on me. I need to be the best to be able to reach the kids. I really do."

Jill said, "I know. I will miss you, hon." Jill gave Eli a massive hug, cried, and let him go.

Eli walked out of the house, got in the limo, and headed for the airport. Landing in Fort Lauderdale and getting out of the plain was like walking into heaven. Eli felt the warm, salty air of the Atlantic. He realized that spring training was about to start again.

He walked into the stadium. The same daunting training regimen was before him. He hated running the steps, but he was determined to do it faster and harder than last year. He decides within himself to lift faster and heavier than ever. His secret ambition was always in the forefront of his mind.

Eli felt his hips getting stronger and stronger. As time went on and he worked on conditioning, he realized his pitches were getting faster and faster. Eli could be seen walking around tossing a ball up in the air and catching it when it came down.

Sam came up to him and asked, "Eli, why do you toss that ball up in the air that way?"

"Oh, it's just a way of getting the rhythm in my head. I just keep that song going through my mind, 'Secret Ambition,'" Eli said.

"Father, is this going to be the year for Eli to win it all?" Peter asked.

"Pete, just stay tuned. Watch what I am going to accomplish. Watch how I build my kingdom," the Lord God responded.

April 2, 2018, was the home opener for Los Angeles. Eli took the mound against New York. The first woman president, Helen Johnson, was going to be throwing out the first pitch. Once again, Eli handed her the ball. He winked and smiled.

Thumbnail whispered to Eli, "Go whisper to her and say, 'Well done, good and faithful servant.'"

Eli got a puzzled look on his face, looked up at the crowd, and waved ever so slightly toward his mom and Jill.

President Johnson threw out the first ball and started to walk off the mound. Eli reached over and touched her shoulder. "President Johnson?"

She turned and looked at Eli. "Yes, young man?"

"I feel like I am supposed to say to you, 'Well done, good and faithful servant,'" he said with the love of his heavenly Father in his voice.

"Eli, you are a special man. Thank you," President Johnson stated.

Eli watched as the president of the United States walked off the field.

"Father, that was pretty special!" Pete said.

"Pete, that is nothing compared to the next time they meet," Father responded

"Next time? What do you mean?" Pete asked.

"Pete, it has to do with kingdom building," Father stated.

Eli took the mound. He could hear the drums, felt the guitar and the piano. The song by Michael W. Smith, "Secret Ambition," was going through his mind. He looked down at the catcher and looked for the sign, which was a fastball straight across. Eli nodded, wound up, and threw. Strike one. Matt Smith, Eli's catcher, signaled for a second fastball low and inside. Eli nodded. He delivered it at 101 miles per hour. The batter was not even close.

"Father, this is going to be a fun season. We are going to watch your greatness mature tremendously in Eli," Pete said.

"Pete, wait 'til you see what I do with Sam. It's going to be even greater for him," Father responded.

"Father, what do you mean?" Pete asked.

"Wait and see. Just wait and see," was the answer Pete got.

Eli pitched eight innings and struck out twenty-four batters before getting pulled. He looked at his manager and asked, "Why would you pull me? I was hot!"

Eli looked at the end of the dugout and saw his father standing there. Ron walked up to Eli.

"I love you, son," he said and hugged him. "Eli, I was wrong. You are one of the greatest pitchers in history. I want what you have," Ron said with tears in his eyes.

"Dad, it is Christ. You know it is Christ. Why don't you stop running from Christ?" Eli stated emphatically.

"Eli, you know that I am Catholic. That is enough religion for me," Ron responded.

"Dad, there is no one who is more Catholic than I am. But if you don't have a personal relationship with Christ, it does not matter. Without having the personal, intimate relationship with Christ, it is all an empty shell," Eli said.

His dad walked away, shaking his head. He just did not get it. Eli wiped away a tear that was running down his face. Having that dynamic relationship with Christ, his heart broke.

The next day, Eli got a phone call from his dad. "Eli, I cannot deny what you have. Let's have coffee."

"Dad, come over to the house. I will have coffee ready when you get here," Eli answered.

"Eli, I don't know where you live," Ron stated with a question in his voice.

"Oh yeah! It is fifteen thirty-five Pacific Coast Drive, apartment two thirty-five."

Two hours later, his dad drove up to the entryway to the complex where Eli lived.

The guard at the gate asked, "Yes, sir. Who can I call for you?"

"Eli McBrien, please."

"Who may I say is calling?" the guard asked.

"His dad," came the answer.

"Father, is Eli going to lead his dad to your son?" Pete asked.

"Pete, stay tuned. This is going to be good," Father responded.

Eli's dad asked, "Eli how do I get to your apartment."

"Dad, give me a minute. I will be right there."

Ron saw Eli walking out in his pajamas. Ron shook his head and said to himself, "This kid will never change. He always has had trouble with mornings."

"Morning, Dad. Great to see you!" Eli said.

"Eli, I hope you have coffee ready. I could really use a cup this morning," Ron stated.

"You know I do, Dad. My housekeeper has it ready for us."

"Housekeeper?" Eli's dad replied.

"Yeah, Dad. I feel like Father has given me a great income, so I do things to put people to work," Eli responded.

As the two men walked up to the apartment, the discussion goes from baseball, to fishing, to his mom and his brothers.

"Eli, your wedding is in June. How are you going to balance baseball with a wedding and a honeymoon?" his dad asked.

Eli responded, "The team has been great! They are giving me an extra day in the rotation."

Then Eli asked the question that has been burning in his heart. "Dad, will you be my best man?"

Ron's jaw dropped. "Of course!" Then his dad changed the subject. "Eli, when we were in the dugout, you told me that an intimate personal relationship with Christ is what makes the difference in all aspects of your life. Can you explain that?"

"Dad, it is like this. I have the Word on my mind in one way or the other all the time. I have Christian music going through my mind continuously. When I am in a jam, there always seemed to be words in my ears from somewhere to bail me out."

With that statement, Thumbnail jumped with glee. "That's me! That's me! When he hears those words, that's me!"

"Eli, are you still driving the Challenger?"

"Dad, that car has caused me so much trouble."

"Mechanical?"

"Not at all. It runs great! The problem is the attention it draws to me."

"Oh yeah," Eli's dad replied.

"The first date with Jill, I got pulled over and it cost me two hundred and fifty dollars in fines. But I learned a lesson."

"The lesson was?" asked Eli's dad.

"Don't hug the wrong curve," replied Eli.

"What?" Ron asked.

"It is a long story. I will explain later," Eli said. "Dad, are you ready to take the step toward intimacy with Christ?"

"Eli, you know that I am."

"Pray after me," Eli said.

With that, Eli led his dad in a prayer of commitment to Christ.

"Eli, I feel clean. For the first time in years, I feel clean!" his dad said, almost yelling.

Eli asked the question. "Dad, it's great that you feel clean, but what are you going to do with it? Dad, I am fed in many different ways. Of course in the Mass, but also by what other pastors and teacher shared. Dad, it was written in First Corinthians 3:1-3 that we must step beyond just taking in the milk of the Word. We have to start growing in the Word. We must also grow by the meat of the Word.

We have to become the Christian that is well grounded in the Word of God. We must not compromise on that which we know is right."

Ron looked over at his son. He knew in his heart he was right. He asked Eli, "Son, could you tell me what the next step is on the journey I have just started?"

Eli asked one simple question. "Dad, how well do you know the word now?"

"Eli, let's just say I know John 3:16. Man I have a long way to go," Ron said.

Ron then asked his son a question that Eli had a bit of a problem answering. "Eli, how did you gain this intimate relationship with Jesus Christ?"

Eli thought for a long moment before he answered. "Dad, remember me telling you about Mom's new friend."

"Yeah?" his dad answered.

"Dad, he laid hands on me and prayed for me. When he did that, I felt something happen inside of me. I felt something warm and comforting enter my heart. I had to read the Bible. The words of the book seemed to come alive. I found myself listening to more and more Christian music. The more I listened, the more I wanted to listen. Even now, I just want to be in Father's presence more and more. When Mom's friend prayed that God's Holy Spirit would come alive in me, I really had no idea what to expect. But this I understand, if we let the Spirit of God indwell us we will do great things. If we work hard building on the talents he has given us there is nothing that he cannot accomplish through us."

Ron looked at his son. "Will you lay hands on me like your mom's friend did for you?"

Eli smiled at his dad as the tears ran down his cheeks. "Dad, of course I will lay hands on you and pray for the Spirit of the most high God totally indwell you."

With that Eli laid hands on his dad. What Ron was about to find out was his life would be changed forever.

The phone rang the next day. "This is Eli. Can I help you?"

"Eli, Sam here. Are you sitting down?"

"What's going on?" Eli asked.

"I just got all of my youth group and yours seats for the surfing contest down in San Diego. We are off those days so we can fly them down. The team says we can use the plane. The kids will love it!" Sam said with shear excitement in his voice.

The next day, they had a game in Minneapolis. Scott Baird, the newest pitcher in the lineup, had a great day. He allowed only two runs while Los Angeles collected five runs.

As the month of April came to a close, Los Angeles was sitting in first place in the division.

The day in June when Eli would wed his sweetheart was drawing closer. Eli found he was on the phone about different things having to do with the wedding over and over again. Jill was getting Eli's approval on everything.

Jill called Eli on a morning when he was getting ready to pitch against the Brown Sox of St. Louis. "Eli, when are you going to be able to get a hands-on for the final arrangements for this wedding?" Jill pleaded.

"Babes, I told you when you wanted a June wedding that it was during the regular season and I would be tied up as far as helping with arrangements. I have been there every time you have called. I have listened to every detail every time you have called."

"Yes, but you never give me any ideas for anything."

"My dear, that's because I trust you. I asked you before if you wanted my help figuring out color schemes, and you turned me down."

"Eli, you and I both knew that you are colorblind and that would be hopeless."

"You are right. One thing. I don't want pink on any part of the tux."

"Got it," Jill answered.

"How's the money holding out? Do you need more?" Eli asked.

"We are fine. I still have over a hundred thousand dollars," Jill answered.

"Are you having fun?" Eli asked.

"Eli, actually I feel like a princess being able to have the wedding of my dreams."

Eli responded, "I have the honeymoon set up. We leave Sunday morning. It will be short because I have to be back to pitch on Thursday. But that will give us a few days just to lay back."

The next day, Eli was pitching. The Phoenix Hornbucklers managed to get two hits off of Eli. One was a homer, and one was a single. Los Angeles won 2 to 1.

At the press conference, Eli was asked what went through his mind on the mound. Eli answered, "I like one particular song that has a real beat to it."

A female reporter asked Eli, "What song is it?"

Eli answers, "It was Michael W. Smith's 'Secret Ambition'"

The reporter followed up, "I know that song. It has a strong beat and a real message. What was your secret ambition?"

"That's an interesting question. If I answered it, then it would no longer be a secret," Eli answered.

Sam leaned over to Eli and asked, "Do you really have a secret ambition?"

Eli just smiled and shrugged as he walked away.

May 15, 2018, was the day Eli is scheduled to pitch against the Louisville Sluggers.

Thumbnail was beside himself. He asked, "Father, it feels like you have something planned for today, but I have no idea what it is."

"Thumbnail, relax. You get so uptight. Today, Eli is going to do something that he did not think he was capable of. But then his whole career will be made up of things he is not capable of doing."

"Father, what is that?" Thumbnail asked.

"Thumbnail, you are going to have to wait and find out like everyone else. It will happen only once in his career, and today is the day."

The national anthem played. Eli took the mound immediately afterward. He looked at Matt and felt power like he had never felt it before.

Mark "The Bomber" Thompson walked to the plate. He gave Eli a big, toothless grin. "Hey, Christian boy, your God is a joke. Today I will show you real power," Thompson yelled.

Eli shook his head, smiled, and tossed the ball into the air. Eli thought to himself, *I can get this guy. I will give him a three-quarter fastball and see what he does with it.* Eli went into his windup, threw the pitch, and it crossed the plate at about eighty miles per hour.

Thompson came around early and drove it out of the park, a foul.

Eli had an expression on his face that was priceless. The surprise of that hit really caught him off guard. Matt signals for an inside curve. Eli nodded and threw the curve. The bomber got a hold of it and drove it out of the park in the opposite direction. It foul was again.

Eli looked at Thompson and thought of David and Goliath. *"Not by might, but by my spirit," says the Lord.* Eli looked up to heaven and prayed, "Father, just once, just this once, make me throw this ball so fast no one can see it. There are kids out here who heard him mock what You have created. Just make this ball go so fast no one can see it."

Eli wound up and threw as hard as he could. That ball was so fast it was not visible to the naked eye. The radar gun had it at 140 miles per hour. The umpire caught a glimpse of the white as it went right down the middle of the plate. Matt jumped up and threw off his glove. He started shaking his hand in pain. Thompson was called out on strikes.

Thumbnail said to Eli, "Yell it!"

Eli yelled, "'Not by might, not by power, but by my spirit,' says the Lord. You have just seen what God can do."

The rest of the game saw Eli giving up three hits and a total of one run. But Los Angeles was held scoreless, and Eli took his first loss of the season.

Henderson, the manager, walked up to Eli. "Look, you pitched a great game. Don't get down on yourself. People are going to get hits off of you."

Pete asked, "Father, why did you let Eli lose? You said you always win."

"I do, but Eli is not me. I had to keep him humble."

Eli said to Henderson, "I think I learned a valuable lesson. Pride really does come before destruction."

Henderson smiled, knowing that Eli finally had it right.

"See, Pete, the lesson was learned. I win again," The Great I AM stated.

The next day, the second game in the series is with the Bombers. Eli sat in the dugout, watching as the Bombers were able to get hits off the other LA pitchers.

Henderson walked over to Eli. "Eli I want you to start talking to the pitchers about watching the batters' stances. Start showing the other pitchers what to look for with these batters."

Eli walked over to talked to Jawaski, the newest pitcher on the team. "Tom, I think if you watch the stances of the next three batters, you can get strikeouts."

"Eli, how do you figure?" Tom asked.

"Watch Thompson. If his feet are parallel, that means he is going to swing away. If the right foot was back, he is going to try to pull it to the left. If the left foot was back, he will pull to the right. With him, you need to keep the ball at his knees. Also, he was a sucker for the changeup."

"What about Smith?" Tom asked Eli.

"Well, Smith is a strange case. I had success yesterday throwing him a screwball."

Eli pulled out the roster and went through each batter with Tom.

"Father, Eli is really learning teamwork here, is he not?" Pete asked.

"Pete, more than that, he is learning what it means to be a servant leader. One other thing he is about to learn is who he is not. I am going to use Jill to show that to him. Next week is the week before his wedding. Watch what happens," Father said.

The next week being the week before the wedding, Jill was going totally bonkers with all of the crazy stuff that had to be taken care of before the wedding. Jill called Eli.

"Eli, can you help me? I have all these things to get done. There is not enough time in the day. I need your help!"

"Jill, I would love to help, but I am important to this team right now. Things are heating up, and I have to be here."

The anger in Jill's voice totally caught Eli off guard. "Look, mister. You need to go to the nearest music store and buy the CD by Casting Crowns 'Who I Am Not.' It is an old song, but you need to hear it."

Eli looked at Henderson standing right behind him. "Eli, why did you agree to a June wedding? She had to know that in the middle of the season, it would be a tough time to get married."

Eli said, "It was the blue eyes. Her dream had always been to have a June wedding."

Henderson looked at Eli and shook his head. "I know that the front office is not going to let me just give you two weeks off. We can't lie and say you are hurt to give you extra time off. What I am going to do could cost me my job. After I do it, you will understand."

Henderson took Eli's hand as if he were going to shake it, squeezed hard, and then brought his knee up into Eli's groin as hard as he could. He twisted the hand harder and hit Eli with a right cross to the jaw.

Henderson asked, "Eli, are you hurt?"

"Yeah. My wrist feels like it is sprained at the least. I will be speaking in a high voice for a week, and you might have broken my jaw."

"Good. You are on injured reserve for two weeks. Now, get out of here."

Eli asked, "You are serious?"

"Yes! Get out of here!"

Eli walked out of the office. The team doctor caught him at the door. "Hold it, McBrien. Let me take a look at that wrist. Henderson just called me and told me you twisted it in his office. I need to check things out before you can go on injured reserve."

The doctor took Eli's wrist and twisted it hard. Eli let out a scream.

"Yes, it is sprained all right. See you in a couple of weeks."

The team jet was waiting on the tarmac for Eli. Eli walked up to it. The team senior owner, Big Russ, was waiting at the jet for him.

"McBrien, I know what has happened here. I am docking you a week's pay and giving you a fine of ten thousand dollars for not being more careful in Henderson's office. He would not tell me what you did, but it had to be really stupid. When I see your bride, I get a kiss, okay?"

Eli answered, "I think that can probably be arranged."

It took ten minutes for the plane to get off the ground.

Eli thought to himself, *I hope nobody told Jill that I* was *flying in today.*

Eli landed at the air base. Nathanial, Eli's big brother, was there waiting with the Challenger, as planned, from their earlier phone conversation. Eli got in the driver's seat. He was ready to jump on the gas when the lights went on behind him.

"No! I just think about driving this car, and cops are all over the place."

"Relax, Eli," Nathanial answered quickly. "These guys are going to escort us to the house."

Eli let out a huge sigh. They drove the fifteen miles from the air base to the house in seven and a half minutes. The police let Eli go alone as he got off the ramp. Eli cruised up to the house, walked in, and heard Jill yell at Nathanial, "Where did you go with Eli's car? He will kill you!"

Eli responded, "Uh, babes."

"Eli!" Jill screamed. She flew across the room, threw her arms around his neck, and hugged him like he had not been hugged before. Jill went limp in his arms and cries. "Eli, how did you get the time off?"

"I hurt my wrist."

"How? In a game?"

"Top secret, and no, I can't tell you."

The extra week passed quickly. Eli listened to Los Angeles lose because Simpson, the pitcher taking his place, lost. He got knocked out of the park.

"Father, they lost because their strongest link was replaced by the weakest link. Eli is doing the right thing by being here. Yet, they lost," Pete said.

"Pete, that is a minor setback in the whole scheme of things. They will be rewarded for taking the steps they did. Remember who is in control here," Father responded.

Eli walked into the living room and threw a pillow from the couch across the room.

Jill looked at Eli. "What is wrong, hon?"

"They blew the game! I should have been pitching in that game, and they blew it!" Eli yelled.

Jill strongly said, "Eli, stop it! You are going to have to make choices all through your life. Will it be your family or baseball?"

"You know, when you put it that way, I guess there is only one thing to do. Babes, I surely do love you," was the only response Eli could give.

"Eli, you are going to be a great husband, father, and the greatest pitcher ever to walk on the field. You can have all three. Just remember where all that greatness comes from," Jill cooed.

"Babes, you are the second greatest thing that ever happened to me!" Eli said in a very loving voice.

Jill got a little grin on her face. "What, mister, is number one?" she responded.

"Christ, of course!" Eli answered with great enthusiasm.

Their eyes met. Eli really, really wanted to kiss her.

Jill thought to herself, *I won't stop him.*

Eli shook his head. "I can't. I won't break my word to your father. I won't."

On Friday night, Nathanial had a bachelor party planned. He had hired a dancer to jump out of a cake. The dancer's name was Jill. Nathanial had been working on this for three weeks. Jill told Nathanial that it wouldn't work. "Eli will have a fit if he saw me jump out of the cake with the bikini that you want me to wear," Jill said. Then she got an angry look on her face. "Nathanial, Eli and I have dated with a sense of purity and holiness from the start. We have committed this whole relationship to the lordship of Jesus Christ." But I do have an idea. She whispered into Nate's hear and the plan was hatched.

As Friday night came. Nathanial picked up Eli in the Challenger, and off they went to Schmitty's Place, the most exclusive nightclub in International Falls. They had the smokers' room reserved. In the early 1900s, it was the room where the men would separate from their wives so they could talk man talk.

At 11:30 p.m., after they had been playing Texas Hold-'Em for hours, the lights went dim. A huge cake is rolled into the room. Eli started to fume. He had told Nathanial that he did not want anything like this. Nathanial shook his head and said to Eli, "I gave you my word."

As the music started, Eli got red with anger. Slowly, the top of the cake was pushed away and this person started to wiggle out of the cake. At first Eli got a little smirk on his face. Then he started to chuckle a bit. Then he started to laugh harder. Pretty soon every guy in the place was rolling on the floor in laughter. The babe was none other than Aaron Bursa, cousin to Sam Bursa.

Eli got home at 2:20 in the morning and crawled into bed, thinking, *Tomorrow, I wonder how late I will be up.* He quickly fell asleep.

Jill got to bed about the same time, wondering the same thing.

On Saturday morning, the birds were singing, the bees were buzzing, and Eli was doing his usual thing: sleeping like a log.

Leah stuck her head in the door and said, "Eli, get your butt out of bed. You have to get ready and get to the church."

Eli asked, "Shoot. What time is it?"

Leah responded, "It's nine thirty!"

Eli jumped out of bed and ran into the bathroom to take his shower. He came out fifteen minutes later and ran into his room and put his tuxedo on.

His mom had his favorite breakfast ready for him: potato pancakes with real maple syrup and sausage links on the side.

Eli said, "Mom, that was great! Thank you!"

Grace answered, "Anything for my little boy!"

Nathanial had his phone out, taking video of the whole thing.

Eli walked by shaking his head and said, "Nathanial, get a life, will you?"

Nathanial answered, "Eli, this has to be remembered for posterity. The great Eli McBrien got married."

The wedding was going to be held at the Cathedral of Christ the Great. It would be conducted by Father James Carligan and the sermon given by John Smith, pastor of First Assembly Church. The service would be a mixture of a Catholic mass with the worship band from First Assembly Church playing the music.

Before the mass started, Eli, his brother, and his father, as well as some of his teammates from high school, were standing at the altar. Michael W. Smith played a song that stirred up great emotion in the people who had gathered for the wedding.

Eli had handed out to each person in attendance Eli and Jill's combined statement of faith. He said after the statement that he and Jill thanked them all for coming and to please be praying for their secret ambition.

Father looked at Peter and said, "This kind of marriage is my shining hour. People will see the great start kids get when they do things my way."

Peter smiled and nodded.

Michael W. Smith finished his song and walked to his seat. The organist started to play as the bridesmaids come in. Michael then realized that he sat down too quickly and goes back to the podium where he is to stand. The next song he is to sing will be the "Bridal March."

As the song "Friends" started to play, Jill walks down the aisle on her father's arm.

Eli watched with an excitement that he would never come close to having again. The biggest win of his career would not even come close to this.

The priest asked, "Who gives this woman to wed this man?"

"Her mother and I do," Jill's dad answered.

Jill's father looked into Jill's eyes and said, "We give you to him, but you will always be my little girl."

Jill stepped to the altar. Their eyes met as tears ran down Jill's cheeks.

Jill's pastor stepped forward. "You two have been a great example for Christ to all the kids you have worked with. You have done it right. You have maintained purity throughout your relationship. Now you are about to enter into a totally new world, the world of husband and wife, and the world of oneness, of becoming a single person in Christ. I charge you to hold to the vows you are about to make. Truly become that person God intends you to be, to experience the joys that he has for you."

He took their hands in his and prayed, "Father, I pray that you will use these kids to bring greatness to your kingdom, greatness that only comes from you. I pray that as they touch others, they will always feel your Holy Spirit flow from them into the people they touch. In the name of Christ our Savior, amen."

Then the priest led them in their vows. The priest then said, "I now pronounce you husband and wife. You may kiss the bride."

Eli nervously lifted the veil and saw his bride. There were tears in their eyes. Eli kissed her lightly. Then the passion kicked in that had been building for two years. They held each other tightly as both their knees got weak.

After the wedding and pictures, there was a beautiful wedding reception. It included a delicious dinner as well as dancing. As the night went on, Henderson got his kiss on the cheek from Jill and big Russ got a quick peck on the lips for allowing Eli to come back early. The most emotional dance was when Jill danced with her Father and Eli with his mom. As the couples danced in the spotlight, Jill looked into her father's eyes. "Daddy, thank you for making Eli promise not to get physical. He kept his promise. He would not break it even when I wanted him to. He showed me that no matter what, I can trust him. Daddy, I love you and I always will."

As the music stopped, Eli and Jill came together. They looked into each other's eyes, and those in attendance could tell that Eli and Jill just wanted to leave to start their honeymoon. So after the dollar dance was over, they headed out to the Ritz in downtown Duluth. That was where the wedding night took place.

Oh, what a night it was.

Eli's Perfect Days

The days of Eli and Jill's honeymoon quickly ended. On Wednesday, they flew back to Los Angeles so Eli could pitch on Thursday. Landing at LAX, they got up out of first class and walked into the corridor.

The press was all over the place, taking pictures and asking for quotes. Eli stopped and said to the press, "Look, guys. We are just getting back from our honeymoon. If you let us go home without hounding us, I am going to the stadium for the game today. After the game, we will hold a press conference and you can ask us anything you like. Whether we answer is our choice."

To Jill's surprise, the press left. Eli and Jill walked through the airport without further incidence.

"Eli, is your life like this all the time?"

"Welcome to big-time sports, sweetheart."

"Father, can their marriage survive this kind of public scrutiny?" Peter asked.

"Pete, remember who I am. I have everything under control. Tell Thumbnail that I need to see him," Father responded.

"Yes, Father? What do you need of me?" Thumbnail asked as he came into the presence of the Most High God.

"Thumbnail, I want you to be aware even more than you have been of the messages I have been sending you for Eli. He is about to enter into the most exciting sports time of his life. It is going to be filled with glory and heartbreak," Father commands.

Thumbnail got a look of concern on his face. "Heartbreak? Will there be trouble with Jill?"

"No. That is rock solid. Just be aware."

Eli and Jill walked up to their home. Eli turned, puts his finger under Jill's chin, lifts it slightly, and kisses her gently. He unlocked the door and carried his bride across the threshold into their home. "Welcome home, Mrs. McBrien!"

"Eli, this has been wonderful! Could it get any better?" Jill responded.

"Sweetheart, Father has a lot of work for us to do. We just need to keep our focus on him. Everything else will be what Father wants it to be. Remember, that all things work for the good to them who love God and are called according to His purpose," was Eli's answer.

Father said with excitement, "Pete, he's got it!"

Eli and Jill walked out on their upper deck of their home. Tina, the housekeeper, brought coffee for them as they sat on the deck, looking out over the ocean.

There was a knock at the door. Tina answered it.

Henderson, Eli's manager, walked in. "Eli, can you pitch this afternoon? I just had a call from Smith's wife. He is in the hospital with appendicitis."

Eli kissed Jill on the forehead and asked, "Babes, are you going to come and watch?"

"Eli, I would not miss it," Jill cooed.

Eli ran out to the limousine that was waiting.

Jill went into the bathroom and took a shower. She came out, looked at herself in the mirror and said, "You are a blessed woman."

She got dressed and walked outside. There was a stretch limousine sitting in the driveway with all the other wives of the players in it. The driver walked around and opened the door. Jill got in.

Sam's wife was sitting there with a grin on her face. "Jill, these are all our sisters in Christ. This is the traditional welcome to the family."

The tears started to stream down Jill's face. Everyone in the limousine started to hug Jill. On the way to the stadium, they all ate grapes and muffins and shared the greatness of Christ. Jill was allowed to hear the testimonies of how the greatness of God the Father had touched many of the wives of the players in a dynamic way.

Eli walked into the locker room. All was quiet, and the room was dark. Suddenly, the lights came on. Henderson got up on a chair.

"Eli, we want to congratulate you on getting married to such a great woman! However, now it is time to get focused on your job. We have to win just about everything from now on to get into the playoffs."

Eli walked onto the field for the first time as a married man. The crowd started cheering and "Congratulations" was put up on the JumboTron. Eli smiled as he raised his hand in gratitude.

He threw a few pitches and warmed up just a bit more. His arm seemed a bit stiff, so he continued to warm up. Soon, everything was moving the way it was supposed to.

The crowd was wondering if Eli's focus was going to be there.

The first batter, Ron Jacobsen, came up to bat. Eli gave him a wink. Eli was feeling focused like a laser beam on this one. He looked into Matt for the signal, which was a fastball at the knees. Eli nodded. It came in at 100 miles per hour. Jacobsen was not even close. Strike one. A second fastball was thrown for strike two. Matt signaled another and it came even faster. He was out.

Batter after batter could not hit Eli. Eli, on his first day back, pitched a perfect game.

After the game, Eli and Jill took the podium to answer questions from the press. Anderson from United Press asked Jill the first question. "May I call you Jill?" was the first question that was put to Eli's bride.

Her answer surprised them a bit in this age of political correctness. Jill answered, "I prefer a more respectful Mrs. McBrien. I want to make one point here. Today Eli pitched a perfect game. That's not the only thing he did perfectly."

The reporter, sensed the possibility of getting something juicy, asked a follow-up question: "What else did he do perfectly?" he asked in a not-so-respectful tone.

Jill glared down at the reporter like a lioness who just had her cubs kidnapped. "My dad put Eli to a test that lasted two years. Eli promised him something that proved very tough to accomplish. Let me say it had to do with purity during our time dating. By keeping the promise he made to my dad, he was able to show me that no matter what he could be trusted. Like I said, pitching was not the only thing he did perfectly. No more questions."

With that, Eli and Jill walked off the podium.

Jill leaned into Eli and asks, "How did I do?"

"Hon, you could not have done any better."

The next two days, Eli was off. But he was still required to go to the park. Jill decided not to go, as he was not going to be pitching on those days. But midway through the fourth inning, on one of the days Eli was not to pitch, LA got into a real jam. Henderson looked at his roster and decided that he had to stretch Eli farther than he had in the past.

"McBrien, warm it up," Henderson hollered

Eli shrugged and got up. His arm was really stiff because he threw nine hard innings two days ago. Eli thought to himself, *That's why they pay me the big bucks.*

Eli started to throw lightly. His arm just did not want to loosen up. He threw and threw, but his arm was really tight. There was an ache in his shoulder that just did not feel right. LA was retired. Eli took the mound. It was the bottom of the ninth, and he had three batters to get out. Eli called time, and had Matt come to the mound.

"Matt, my shoulder is really sore. I just don't understand it. Let's try to finesse these guys a bit. If I have to come with the heat, I will, but, man, I just don't know."

The first batter he got out with a curve, a screwball, and a changeup. The second fell for a sinker, a screwball, and a changeup. The third batter had it figured out. Eli knew it. So he hit him with three fastballs in a row, and the game was done.

After the game, Eli went into the team doctor. He explained what was going on. The doctor ordered an MRI on Eli and saw something he did not like. He sent Eli to the hospital for more tests. Eli went through a battery of tests. They checked range of motion, they checked strength, they ran more MRIs. Hour after hour went by. Test after test was completed. The nurse finally came in and told Eli the tests were over.

The doctor came in and said, "Eli, I have never seen this before. Arthritis in a twenty-year-old kid is almost unheard of. It is like your arm has been working so hard that the joint is really getting worn out."

"Doc, am I going to do more damage to it if I keep pitching?"

"Eli, we are going to have to see what it looks like. But the best bet would be not to pitch anymore."

Eli asked, "If I do?"

"You can probably get through this season. But after that, who knows?"

"Looks like I have a decision to make," Eli said. As he walked toward his car, he was thinking to himself, *I need to get home and pray with Jill. I really need to pray with Jill. I really need Father's guidance on this.*

No sooner had Eli climbed into the Challenger than his phone rang. It was Henderson. "Eli, the doc just called me. We have a good shot at the series. If you decide to play, I will use you in a limited role. What that looks like, I am not sure yet. I was thinking of starting you every third week. I would use you in the bullpen for the rest of the time. Go home and think about it, maybe even pray about it," Henderson said.

Eli went home.

Jill met him at the door. "You are late, hon. What happened?"

"Oh, they ran a bunch of tests on my shoulder and found arthritis."

"Eli, aren't you a bit young for that?" Jill asked as she put the finishing touches on their steak dinner that she had been preparing.

"I have been throwing really hard for a long time. I guess the bones didn't like it."

Jill asked, "What was the prognosis?"

"Well, if I keep pitching this year, there is no guarantee that I will be back next season. If I don't pitch the rest of this year, there is no guarantee for next season," Eli answered.

"So what are you going to do?" Jill asked.

"Jill, let's pray about this," Eli said. Eli and Jill spent the next thirty minutes holding each other's hands while they prayed about the situation.

Thumbnail finally got the word from the great I AM.

"Eli, it's time to play ball. Remember your secret ambition. You were placed here for such a time as this." Thumbnail spoke directly into Eli's ear.

Jill looked at her beloved and said, "Eli, we both know what you have to do. We both know that this is a one-time deal. Father is going to use us in ways we just cannot imagine. But somehow he did not bring us this far to let us fall. It's not a time to quit, but keep pushing on."

Eli answered, "I agree, hon. We have a real shot at the World Series this year. We have to live today, as Scripture says. I am going to play. Henderson is going to start me only every third week. I will pitch relief the rest of the time," Eli answered.

That night, as Eli and Jill were driving back to their exclusive neighborhood in suburban LA, they were driving through downtown Los Angeles. They made a wrong turn and ended up in a ghetto. Suddenly, their car was surrounded by gang members who looked like trouble. Eli got on his cell phone, dials 911, and turns on the GPS on his phone.

Suddenly, the leader of the gang figured out that this was Eli and Jill. He said, "Guys, we have got to get this car out of here. This is Eli McBrien, that new pitcher for LA."

Another member walked up to the car and spit on Jill. Eli just about came out of the car when the leader pulled him aside and whispered something to him.

Eli reached into the back seat of his Challenger, grabbed his Bible, and got out of the car. Eli got on the hood of his car and started to preach. "You guys want to win. You really want to win. I am holding here in my hand the most powerful weapon in the world," Eli shouted.

One of the gang members shouted, "Yeah. I'm scared that Bible is going to take me down."

Eli could hear Thumbnail as he yelled into Eli's ear the words that Eli needed to say to the gang.

Eli looked at the gang member. "This does not win by killing. It wins by rebuilding lives. It wins by taking a destroyed person and giving them hope."

One of the gang member asked, "How can that book give this boy hope?"

Eli answered with even more power, "It gives hope through the risen Christ!"

The gang leader hopped up on the roof with Eli. "Listen, brothers, this boy speaks the truth! I can see it in his eyes." With that, he turned to Eli, "Look. You know and I know I saved your butt here. You come back in the off season and share your Christ with us. You have something we need," Jamaal said.

Eli answered, "I give you my word. I'll be back, and I will bring some other players with me."

Eli got in the car, opened the glove box, and grabbed twenty tickets to the game next week. He got the attention of the leader and asked, "What's your name?"

"Jamaal," the leader quickly answered.

"Here are twenty tickets to the next game when I am pitching. I will let security people know you are coming. These are box seats. You'll like them," Eli said.

The next week, Eli was getting ready to pitch against Seattle. The phone rang in the locker room a half hour before the team got ready to take the field.

"Eli, there is a Jamaal up here. He says you gave them these box seat tickets to the game. Is that correct?"

"It sure is. Make sure they eat well during the game, would you?" Eli responded.

So the stadium brought in all kinds of food. There were hamburgers, hotdogs, soda, ice cream, anything they wanted.

Eli pitched a two-hitter through eight innings. They won 3 to 1.

After the game, the gang members were brought into the locker room. Eli showed them around. He introduced them to Sam, who agreed to help Eli with the outreach that was going to help the gang members.

The next day, they were off. Eli and Sam went to their respective churches to talk to them about outreach to the gang members. The results they got were not what they expected. Both suburban churches did not want anything to do with what Eli and Sam were contemplating.

They walked out of their churches asking themselves, "Now what do we do?" They looked at each other in total disbelief. "Our churches have had a mission field handed to them on a platter. They have sent missionaries all over the world, but when Father put one in our back yard, they wanted nothing to do with it," Sam said.

Eli responded, "Bro, I think it's time we just go home, sit down with our wives and spend some time in prayer about this."

The next day Eli called Sam on the phone and said, "I think it's time we find churches that have a heart for the mission they have in their backyard. I think we should go to the local Bible school and find us a young pastor to help us start a church." Eli said.

Sam quickly retorted, "Eli, I can't believe what I have just heard from you. You want to start a Protestant church. This is coming from a Catholic boy?"

"Sam, don't get me wrong. I will always be Catholic. But these kids have to be reached by Christ. Remember, the Word says, 'How can they hear without a preacher'?" Eli said.

"Eli, we have to play for the next three days with this home stand. Let's get busy and put an AD in the school placement office. We will fund it for the first couple of years. Then they should be able to cover their own expenses after that," Sam said.

The next day, Eli took the mound and pitched like a man on fire. A few times a game, the pain would get pretty severe, but Eli would pray through it. "Secret Ambition" would be playing in his mind as he forced himself through the pain. He realized that he had the words that would save hundreds of young people. He knew he had to keep throwing. Their lives depended on it.

Eli threw strike after strike, knowing that young people would listen to what he had to say because of his fame.

He realized that only through Christ could he have the power to accomplish what he had to do with the limited time he had on the mound.

The season was rushing by so quickly. Win after win was pushing LA closer and closer to their goal of the World Series.

Eli and Sam were getting testy at home. But the girls understood what was at stake.

Eli walked out over and over again and pitched strikeouts. He kept praying over and over again to get him through the season. It looked to be coming down to one game, one last game of the season to see who would be playing for the pennant. Colorado had been having a dynamic season. They were going to be the team to beat to take the division.

Los Angeles had to fly out to Denver for the game. Eli tried to sleep on the plane, but sleep just seemed to evade him. This was to be the biggest game to this date. Upon landing in Denver, the bus to take them to the stadium was waiting. Eli was the last one off the plane because he was sitting and praying. The rest of his teammates knew that this was one time not to interrupt Eli.

As his prayer ended, Eli got up out of his seat, reached across with his left arm to his right, and worked his shoulder. Eli looked up to heaven and said, "Father, just get me through this season. Please give me the Series."

"Pete that is something he has to earn. Remember, he has worked his whole life for this. Remember, too, that all good things come from me," Father stated.

As he walked into the stadium, the song "Secret Ambition" started going through his mind. His thoughts went back to the gang being around his car and how the Word of God started to touch their hearts. He wanted and needed to see these guys touched by the power of Jesus Christ and to see them touched in such a way that they could touch all those around them. Eli felt the power of the Spirit fill his whole being. He felt the power that he remembered as an eleven-year-old in the gym with his coach and mom watching.

Eli looked up at heaven and asked, "Father, is this what all of this is about?"

Thumbnail whispered, "You got it, Eli. You got it!"

During warm-ups, Eli's shoulder started to loosen, and he heard the pounding drums, the keyboards, and Michael's voice. It was there. He looked down at Matt. Matt smiled inside his catcher's mask. He had seen this look on Eli before, and he knew that no one was going to hit him this day.

The first batter came to the plate. Eli chuckled to himself. His shoulder was loose. He tossed the ball up and caught it with the music still in his ears. Matt signaled for a fastball. Eli delivered. The poor guy never had a chance.

If Colorado knew what was really going on, they would just pack it up and go home. No one hit Eli McBrien. Not today.

After the game, Jill was waiting for Eli outside the locker room.

As Eli came out, he looked at Jill, saw her smile, and said, "Let's go, hon."

Jill smiled and put her arm through Eli's as they walked out to the car. The drive to the motel was a talkative one. They had Christian music playing in the background. Jill started singing to some of the music. The purity and clarity of her voice, as always, cut right to Eli's heart.

Right then, it hit Eli like a ton of bricks. "Sweetheart, I have an idea. I wonder how many of the other guys on the team who are believers also play instruments. You, my dear, have a great voice. It is pure and sweet, yet one that could bring the message of love and salvation to those who have heard it," Eli said.

The look on Jill's face was one that communicated very clearly her dislike of the idea of singing in public. "Eli, no way am I singing in public. You know how I hate getting in front of people."

Eli reached over and took her hand and said, "Sweetheart, you have been given a gift, as much of a gift as being able to throw a baseball. You need to use that gift for Father's kingdom." As soon as Eli got into the house, he was on the phone. "Matt! You are a drummer, aren't you?"

"Yeah, I am, Eli. What do you need?"

"Matt, I was thinking. If we started a band, it would open doors of ministry to all those kids in the ghetto. What do you think?"

"You know, Eli, I like the idea. We have been blessed out of our socks here. But who will be the lead singer? I have heard you in the shower, and there is no way you can do it. Sam plays a pretty mean bass guitar. Let's see if we can get him to join us."

"You have got to hear Jill! I am amazed by her voice!" Eli said excitedly.

After a couple more phone calls, four of them were sitting in Eli's living room, discussing plans for the band. Jill walked over to the keyboards and started doing an old Amy Grant number. The guys looked at each other. Matt and Sam's eyes got wide with amazement. They smiled.

We have our band. Now let's see what Father has for a message for us to deliver to those who need to hear it.

The next two weeks, however, were going to be a total bust as far as putting together a game plan for the ministry. Eli and Sam left it to the girls to gather résumés from young men willing to help build a new church in the ghetto.

Meanwhile, the guys realized that to get into the World Series, they had to win three out of five games against New York, who has not been to the World Series in decades.

Henderson, the manager, walked up to Eli. "Look, Eli, this might be a one-shot deal with you and that shoulder. You have worked for this your whole life. How do you want to play it?"

Eli rotated his shoulder. He knew the speed he could throw. He also knew the pain that would be there. He thought of the pain Christ went through two thousand years ago. Eli looked up to heaven and prayed silently, *Father, the kids need this. You have created me for such a time as this. Let's get it done.* Eli looked at Henderson and said,

"I will give you everything I have left. There is more going on here than you could possible understand. Assuming we make the World Series, my attorney wants two tickets and I need twenty of the same box seat tickets for those gang members."

Henderson looked at Eli. "You get me two games in the next Series and you've got your tickets."

Eli arrived at home around six from the light workout the team had. He had Jill put warm compresses on his shoulder to soothe the joints. The feel of her sweet hands messaging his sore shoulder was heaven to Eli. The more she massaged, the less pain was there. "I sure do love you, babes. I don't know what is left of this baseball career that Father has placed me in. But this I do know: as long as I have breath, I will use the gifts that Father has given me to reach these kids. I feel the Spirit within me driving me to be better and better. I feel the spirit within me driving me to be the one who Father uses to touch all those kids. All I want to hear is well done good and faithful servant. All I want to see are these kids lives changed by the power of the spirit of the Most high God," Eli said.

Jill rubbed his shoulder for a few more moments, reached down, kissed Eli on the cheek, and said, "I really do love you too, sweetheart."

The next day, Eli met with the trainer, who told Eli, "We could give you cortisone shot to save you from some of the pain in the next game. Would you like me to do that? It is a temporary fix to something that is going to affect you for the rest of your life."

Eli responded, "Let me make a phone call. I will get back to you." Eli got on the phone to his doctor in Roseau. "Tom, Eli McBrien here. I have arthritis in my right shoulder, and it is getting pretty sore."

Tom answered before Eli could ask the question. "Are they offering you cortisone shots for the games you have to play?"

"Yes, they are, Tom. I just wanted your opinion."

"Take the shots. Next season, though, you might have trouble," Tom said.

Tom didn't know that there would be a next season. He realized that the extent of the injury to the shoulder must be very extensive for them to have to use cortisone to enable Eli to throw.

Eli walked back into the locker room and said, "Give me the shot."

After the shot, Eli started to work his shoulder. He looked over at the doctor and smiled.

The doctor said, "Eli, this is not a painkiller. It is a lubricant."

"McBrien, phone," one of his teammates hollered.

"Hello. McBrien here. Can I help you?"

"Eli, this is Jamaal. I have a buddy here who is really into drugs. Could you talk to him?"

"Could you bring him to the stadium in about half an hour? I have to pitch batting practice, and then I will have some free time," Eli responded.

The cortisone shot worked wonders. Eli was able to throw hard yet with very little pain. He looked up to heaven and gave thanks.

"Pete, I have everything under control. I did not want him taking Novocain but needed him to be able to throw," Father stated lovingly.

"Father, could you not have just healed his shoulder?" Pete asked.

"Pete, people don't understand. I work all things for the good. It's better if I don't heal Eli. What I am bringing him into has a much greater impact for my kingdom than if I left him on the baseball field," Father answered.

"McBrien, security called. There are a couple of gang members to see you. Have you got time for trash?"

An immediate flash of anger crossed Eli's mind. "Look, Schmidt. Change a couple of things in our lives and we are there! Tell security to send them in."

Jamaal and his friend came into the locker room. The friend looked really rough. He has been doing meth for a couple of years, and it had had a bad effect on him.

Jamaal looked at Eli with a look that said, "Man, you're our last hope."

Eli called the team doctor over. "What do you suggest we do? This kid is in a bad way."

The team doctor had a light go on inside his brain. (Actually it was Thumbnail whispering in his ear.) The doctor got on the phone, called the team's owner, came back, looked at the kid, and said, "Look. Los Angeles is willing to help you with this. They will pay for your treatment. But in return, you tell your story and give the team the credit for accomplishing something great in you. The owner is going to be setting up a scholarship to do this for one kid a year."

Eli and Jamaal looked at each other. Jamaal said, "That was the best wrong turn you ever made!"

Eli responded, "With Christ, there are no wrong turns!"

The young man was then sent to an exclusive treatment center as one of the team's associates.

That night, the team had to catch a plane. Their charter was winging its way to New York. Jill was in the back of the plane with all of the other wives. Eli had his headphones on and was in a state of constant prayer throughout the flight.

Landing in New York, there was a limousine that took all the wives to the Ritz Carlton. The players had a team meeting and a meal. The team pastor said a prayer, and the men met their wives for a relaxing evening.

The next morning, they were up early to head for the field. In the locker room, Eli was praying. He was praying for the guys he was going to beat and for the safety of himself and the other players.

The team doctor gave Eli his cortisone shot. Then Eli went out on the field to warm up. He walked out on the field and heard the music start. Michael W. Smith was in his head. He knew what his secret ambition was and what he was going to do—and what he had to do to see it completed. He looked down from the mound at Matt. Eli knew the course this game was going to take. He threw and threw and threw inning after inning. Only one batter was able to hit him.

Henderson smiled but also had the sense that this series is going to be Eli's last. He understood what was going on in Eli's shoulder. But for this season, for a time such as this, Eli McBrien was going to be the best there has ever been.

Between innings, Henderson walked up to Eli. "How is the shoulder doing?"

"It feels okay. I am having fun. This is great! I feel like a kid again!"

The fourth inning saw Los Angeles score four runs giving them a three-run lead.

Eli's speed usually meant if the opposing team was able to get a hit, it would be a home run.

Eli looked into Matt's eyes. Matt knew what was going on. He knew the pain that every throw meant. Even though the shots were helping, the pain was still there.

Batter after batter, strikeout after strikeout, brought them closer and closer to the World Series that was set for such a time as this.

Finally, the ninth inning came and went. This would be Eli's last full game ever. Eli knew it. As the last pitch was thrown, he stood on the mound with his mind going back to the last pitch as a high school pitcher. His mind went to what it was all about. It came down to this: reaching the kids. Eli sensed the same short depression, knowing he would never again pitch a full game. He leaned over picked up a handful of dirt and blew it off of his hand with the wind at his back. He looked to heaven and simply prayed a prayer of thanks for the great memories he had from that mound.

Eli got the win.

Being scheduled to pitch in game five, if necessary, Eli was really hoping it would not go that far. He got a call to pitch one inning in game three to seal that game, giving Los Angeles a two-to-one lead in the series.

Flying back to Los Angeles gave Eli and Sam a chance to talk about the ministry for the first time. The girls have been on the phone in the evening and have found an old church that can be purchased for a relatively small amount of money.

Game four went to New York, as Los Angeles just could not seem to get it together in the hit department. So it came down to game five.

Eli was in the locker room. The team doctor gave him his cortisone shot. Eli went off to a corner to pray by himself. Eli prayed, *Father, this is one step. Your son suffered and died so that we could live. I can give one more here to get a step closer.*

Once again, "Secret Ambition" went through his head. He smiled as he walked out on the diamond. This is it!

Eli took a few pitches to warm up. Matt could see the focus, knowing instinctively that it was Eli's game. The first three innings, no one even got close. In the fourth, someone got a base hit, and then the next three went down in order.

Eli was relieved in the ninth as Smith ended the game.

Los Angeles managed to get a couple of runs, and the game was over.

They had three days off until the World Series. Eli was grateful, as he would be able to give his arm a much-needed rest.

Back in Los Angeles, the girls had three résumés for the guys to look at. Eli looked at Sam and Matt, and they saw the résumé of Stuart Johnson.

"How about a building?" Sam asked with concern.

Sam's wife, Corrine, answered, "We found an old Baptist church that we have already bought for a song. We are set."

The two families contributed $250,000 for the pastor's salary and the first year's operation.

There was a knock at the door.

Eli rose to answer it. Eli opened the door and said, "Can I help you?"

"Oh, Eli, this is Stuart. I forgot he was coming over to meet you," Jill said.

"Mr. McBrien, it is a pleasure to meet you," Stewart said.

Eli asked, "So you think you could help us reach these kids?"

"Yes, sir, I do. But I understand that you and Sam have had some experience with youth."

Sam jumped in. "We do, but to be honest, not at this level and with this many problems."

Stuart asked, "When do you gentlemen and ladies want to start this church?"

Eli answered, "How about November first, right after the World Series ends?"

Stuart continued, "You do understand that I am from Duluth, Minnesota, and don't have a lot of experience with the ghetto either."

"Let's just see what happens," Eli answered with total confidence.

With that, everyone left.

The End Is the Beginning

The World Series.

Games one and two of the World Series were going to be played in Minnesota.

In game one, Henderson walked up to Eli and said, "Can you give me your best today?"

"Tom, I was created for such a time as this, and I won't be beat!"

Eli walked out with strong, cold determination on his face and the music playing in his ears. He looked at Rucket and threw hard and fast for three pitches, and down Rucket went.

Eli went through six innings with his shoulder getting more and more sore. He kept throwing. He got into the eighth inning. Now he had to work combination pitches to get Minnesota's batters out.

Sam came up to bat for Los Angeles and hit a grand slam.

At the beginning of the ninth inning, Henderson pulled Eli. As Eli walked off the field, he handed the ball to Henderson, who handed it to Jacobsen, his regular closer. Jacobsen made short work of the rest of the order, striking each man out as he came up to bat.

The game ended with Los Angeles winning the game.

However, the next game was not as pretty, with LA getting wiped out with a score of 8 to 1. Rucket had his usual hot day, driving in four with a grand slam.

After the game, Eli and Sam took some time to get together and make extensive plans for the ministry Father was about to start in the ghetto.

Eli and Sam drove through the ghetto. Then they stopped and got out and started walking down the street praying. They asked Father what they should be doing.

They brought the girls in when they got home. The wives could see the concern and hurt on Sam and Eli's face.

They asked together, "What is wrong with you guys?"

Sam responded, "We walked through the ghetto today. We saw kids with no hope and no clue as to what was going on. We knew if we could bring Christ to them, their future could be better."

The next day, Minnesota came to Los Angeles. They had a three-game home stand. Having lost a game in Minnesota, Los Angeles needed to win three to win the World Series. But they were unable to do it.

Los Angeles won two and lost one, giving them a three-to-two lead in the World Series.

Los Angeles went back to Minnesota and lost the first game.

They got into the seventh and final game of the World Series. Eli walked up to Henderson and said, "If you want to start me, I can get you a win."

"Eli, I can't, in good conscience, start you. I can't. Trust me on this one. I know when I will use you. I am starting Thomas."

"Oh, Eli, your buddies from the ghetto are here. I put them in the suite. They are in heaven," Henderson said.

Thomas looked great through the first eight innings. Being a finesse pitcher, he was able to keep their best hitters at bay.

Eli was praying, *Father, if I don't play, that's your choice. But I want this game.*

In inning nine, Los Angeles was up by one run with no outs. Thomas seemed to have lost control and loaded the bases.

MPLS Gazette *Sports*, October 2018

It was a classic showdown between Minnesota and Los Angeles in the Metrodome. No one could understand why we were now in game seven of the World Series and Eli McBrien had not been seen since game one when he struck out twenty-four batters in eight innings. Jon Thomas loaded the bases in the bottom of the ninth. There were no outs. Now, Todd Rucket, grandson of the late Kirby Rucket, the great outfielder for Minnesota, was up to bat. He had a .400 batting average with thirty-six homeruns during the regular season. Against the Los Angeles pitching staff, he had been making all the pitchers look like rank amateurs. Henderson, LA's managers walked out to the mound. Thomas was seen shaking his head. Eli had been warming up gently through the last inning. His arm seemed a bit sore. But when the game was on the line, they were going to go with their twenty-year-old sensation.

After the game, I asked Eli what went through his mind as he faced the hitter of hitters.

Eli replied, "I looked down from the mound and saw him standing there. Let me tell you, he looked mean. So the first thing I did was ask Christ to touch his heart and draw Rucket to Himself. I then asked the Holy Spirit to guide the ball to where it needed to be."

Well, folks, this is what this reporter saw. Eli threw his first fastball at 109 miles an hour. Rucket fanned it. But then McBrien tried to catch him with his patented changeup. McBrien just about got caught himself. Rucket got a piece of it and drove it out of the ballpark. The ball must have gone four hundred feet. There was one little problem. It was foul.

I could see McBrien give a big sigh of relief as he looked up to heaven. I could almost see his lips say, "Thank you." So now we had two strikes. McBrien knew what he had to throw. The problem was, so did Rucket. Both men knew it was going to be a fastball. They knew this ball would probably be the fastest, hardest ball that McBrien had ever thrown. McBrien looked up at the crowd. He saw his mom sitting there. She looked like she was praying. Everyone in the crowd was silent. They knew that this was the guy to beat. Everyone knew that McBrien could fan the next two batters without a lot of trouble. They knew the last pitch to Rucket was the game. McBrien went into his wind-up. Just before he threw, Rucket called time. He was trying to break McBrien's concentration. Eli stepped away from the mound and tosses the ball up in the air as if to say, "Listen. This is going to smoke you, and there is not a thing you can do about it."

McBrien stepped back on the mound. His foot moved back and forth, kicking the dirt on the pitching rubber. He tossed the ball in the air again and winked at Rucket. Again, his eyes tell Rucket, "You won't even see this." Rucket looked at McBrien as if to tell him, "I am going to send this to the moon!" This is a classic battle. Classic!

McBrien wound- up. Folks, that ball went so fast it was a streak of white. The umpire called strike. Rucket looked and smiled. He walked back to the dugout and raised his right hand in respect.

McBrien fanned the next two batters. This was a classic battle. It will go down in history as one of the greatest match ups of hitter versus pitcher in baseball history.

McBrien won.

There is more to this pitcher than meets the eye. He says it is God. He says it's his faith in Christ.

How do we argue with him?

—Goldy Goldsmith
Freelance Writer
MPLS r Tribune Gazette

This story is to be continued.

Comprehension Questions

Chapter 1 Comprehension Questions

1. Who was the World Series between?
2. Who was the 20-year-old pitcher who had struck out 24 batters in 8 innings?
3. Who was the player with a .400 batting average?
4. What went through Eli's mind as he faced , the hitter of hitters? What did Eli do?
5. What happened when Eli threw Todd Rucket his change-up?
6. Why does the book stop without finishing what happens in the World Series?
7. How old is Eli at the beginning of the story?
8. What was Eli's health problem?
9. What important influence would Eli's mom's friend have on Eli? How was this accomplished?
10. Who taught Eli how to throw a change-up?
11. Who had taught Eli how to play guitar?

12. When Eli is in surgery, what did Eli's mom ask God (Father) to do?
13. How does Grace, Eli's mom, feel while Eli is in surgery?
14. After surgery, how does Eli feel?
15. What other mother felt agony when her son was in tremendous pain?
16. When Eli comes home to his aunt's house, is he still in pain? How do you know?
17. What does Eli's mom do for Eli's pain?
18. Is the prayer helpful? How do you know?
19. Why was this really important for Eli to experience?

Chapter 2 Questions

1. Why does Eli lift weights?
2. How old is Eli now?
3. What gift is God giving Eli at this point?
4. How is Eli going to be used by God?
5. What does Eli realize about his pitching talent?
6. What did Eli use to help him with his pitching?
7. What song would play through his head giving Eli's pitching that much more power?
8. How fast was Eli's fastball traveling?

9. What experience with the varsity team showed that Eli had incredible pitching power?

Chapter 3 Questions

1. Why does the coach ask Eli to slow down his pitching?
2. What was God teaching Eli when He let Hunter hit the ball out of the park?
3. Why did Eli's coach let Eli burn the ball when was pitching to Sam in batting practice?
4. When Sam asks the coach where Eli gets those pitches, what does the coach say?
5. When Eli asks his coach if God would use a young kid like him to do anything, what answer does he get?
6. How is God going to use Eli?
7. What does the varsity coach ask Eli?
8. What happens next?
9. Why does Eli's catcher hate when Eli throws heat?
10. When Ned yelled, "You can't throw fast enough to strike me out," what was he showing?
11. What happened in the game when Ned came up to bat?

Chapter 4 Questions

1. What is the girl's name that is attracted to Eli?
2. How old is Eli now?

3. What happened the night Eli went to church with Jill?

4. What does Father teach Eli? How?

5. When Eli storms off the mound, what does Eli's coach tell him?

6. How does Eli react?

7. What does Eli's coach say?

8. Then, what does Eli ask?

9. What happens when Eli pitches to the Bulldogs best hitter, Todd Johnson?

10. When Eli winks at his mom, what kind of pitch is he going to throw? Why?

11. When Eli and Jill go to youth group, what other talent does Eli share?

12. What does the youth leader say when Jill makes the statement that Eli is Catholic and Eli defends being Catholic?

13. What does Eli say the reason is for his being there?

Chapter 5 Questions

1. Who is on the phone wanting to talk to Eli? About what?

2. What is God going to use Eli to do?

3. How will God keep Eli's pride in check?

4. Where do Eli and Jill go and what are they planning to do for fun?

5. Why does God send angels to be with Eli and Jill?

6. When Eli starts to kiss Jill, what does he see?

7. Why does God send this?

8. What happens to Eli when he was driving the Challenger faster than he should have been?

9. Why does Grace, Eli's mom, call her friend, John, the police officer, back?

10. What does Eli do for the 4th-6th grade kids at Mahomet?

11. What is the award going to be? What is it awarded for?

12. What does Tommy say about Aaron? What happens then?

13. When Tommy's dad returns with Tommy the next week, what happens?

14. Who wins the special award?

Chapter 6 Questions

1. Why is there a meeting with Eli, Eli's mom, Jill, and Jill's parents?

2. How does Aaron react when Eli calls about taking him to the Chicago baseball game?

3. What does Eli explain to Aaron about the batters at the game?

4. What will be the effect on Aaron from the time spent with Eli?

5. What does Eli say is the reason he is working so hard?

6. What happens around the flagpole at the school?

7. What is the littlest angel's name? What is his job?

8. Who did the English teacher cast in the senior play "Romeo and Juliet"?

9. Why does Eli refuse to do the play?

10. What does the teacher say to Eli about not wanting to do the play?

11. Why does Eli call his mom?

12. How does Eli's mom respond?

13. What does Eli's mom tell the English teacher?

14. What does the English teacher tell Eli and Jill after Eli's mom leaves?

15. When Eli's coach asks where the speed in Eli's pitching comes from, what does Eli say?

16. What does the coach say to this?

17. Eli responds with what answer?

18. When Jill tells Eli they should do the play, what does Eli tell Jill?

19. Why does God allow Thumbnail to be washed off Eli's shoulder and almost down the drain?

20. What do the girls from school want Eli to do?
21. Why does Eli refuse?
22. What does Janice, a football cheerleader, do?
23. What does Eli do then?
24. What does the officer do?
25. What does Eli tell him?
26. How is the problem solved?
27. What does Eli do to show his disapproval of how the girls acted?
28. What does Jill start to suggest to Eli as they drive home?
29. How does Eli respond?
30. What does Jill say then?

Chapter 7 Questions

1. Why is Eli sad as chapter 7 opens?
2. What is Eli offered by the Los Angeles farm team?
3. Does Eli accept the contract?
4. How much is he being paid?
5. What does Eli's dad tell Eli about signing the contract?
6. What does Eli's mom tell Eli?
7. What three pitches does Eli have at this point in his career?

8. How does Eli do his first game pitching for the Crystals?
9. Where does Eli go with his catcher after the game?
10. What happens when Chris, the bartender, suggest they get together after work?
11. What happens when a beautiful blond woman walks up to Eli and asks him to buy her a drink?
12. What happens when Jill walks into the bar?
13. What does Jill's dad ask of Eli?
14. What does Eli say?
15. What does Jill's dad ask Eli not to do? Why?
16. What is Eli allowed to do with Jill?
17. When Phil Smith makes a rude comment about Jill, what does Eli do?
18. Why does Eli lose the next game?
19. Eli learns what from this?
20. What does Eli ask Jill's dad?
21. Jill's dad responds how?

Chapter 8 Questions

1. Eli is offered what amount of money to play for the major league team in Los Angeles?
2. How much does Stan, Eli's attorney want as a signing bonus for Eli?

3. How much will the attorney take?

4. What does Eli want to talk to Jill's dad about?

5. What does Jill's dad say?

6. At the airport, what does Eli ask Jill?

7. What does Jill say?

8. What does God tell Pete when someone gives themselves to God, what does God give them?

9. Eli's attorney gets what incentive written into Eli's contract?

10. Before Eli signs the contract, what does he ask the owner of the Los Angeles ball team for?

11. Eli buys what at Tiffany's?

12. When Eli returns to Champaign, what does Eli ask Jill? What does he give her?

13. Thumbnail whispers what to Eli as to how God will use him?

14. What does Eli do to get in shape for the season?

15. Who throws out the first pitch in the opening game for Los Angeles?

16. What song does Eli hear playing in his head as he takes the mound to pitch?

17. Eli has a "secret ambition". What is it?

18. How did Eli pitch in his first major league game?

19. What does Eli tell his teammates is the prize they need to keep their eyes on?
20. Fred Lemue thinks he has figured out how to hit Eli? What is the key to this success?
21. Why does Eli use his fastball stance and then not throw any fastballs to Fred Lemue?
22. When Sam says Eli seems possessed when he works out, what does Eli respond?
23. What happens when Jill tries to get close to the players' gate at the stadium so she can meet Eli when he comes out?
24. When Eli appears, what happens? What does he tell Hank?
25. How much is Jill allowed to spend on the wedding?
26. What are the terms of the contract that Eli is offered?
27. Does he sign it?

Chapter 9 Questions

1. What is the priest's hesitation for a combined youth group with another denomination?
2. Eli says that their purpose for the youth group is what?
3. What does Eli realize is a major issue with a lot of the kids?

4. Eli suggests what as a way to get these kids from the two different churches working together?

5. How will this help bring them together?

6. What was the final question that would decide the winner of the Bible Baseball game? What was it worth?

7. Why was the answer's validity in question?

8. What was the final ruling and why?

9. Where did Sam and Eli decide to take their youth groups on a hayride?

10. Who paid for it?

11. Where would they spend the night?

12. How many kids would there be?

13. Eli's mom's reaction to this was what? Who helped her?

14. What did the kids do on the farm and hayride?

Chapter 10 Questions

1. Why is Eli so devoted to being able to throw a baseball faster and harder than anyone else in the world?

2. Is Eli keeping his word about not kissing Jill until their wedding day? Why?

3. Why does Eli toss the ball up in the air and catch it when it comes down when he is pitching?

4. What does Eli say to President Johnson when she has thrown the first ball out for the opener?
5. Who whispers this to Eli?
6. In 8 innings, Eli strike out how many batters?
7. Eli's dad says what to Eli when he sees him at the ball field?
8. What does Eli say to his dad?
9. How does Eli's dad respond?
10. Eli's response about being "Catholic" is what?
11. What does Eli's dad do then?
12. Why does a tear run down Eli's face?
13. The next day when Eli's dad comes to see Eli, what happens?
14. Jill is getting what help from Eli with the wedding plans?
15. How long will they have for a honeymoon?
16. Why does Father allow Eli to lose the game against the Louisville Sluggers?
17. The week before the wedding, what does Jill ask Eli?
18. How does Eli get the time off?
19. What does Eli have to pay for being injured?
20. Why does Eli get upset when he is with Jill and away from the team?

21. Jill says what to Eli that settles him down?

22. What else does Jill say to Eli?

23. Who is it that comes out of the cake at the bachelor's party? What hides her identity?

24. What does she tell Eli?

25. What is the wedding service a mixture of?

26. The pastor tells Eli and Jill what advice?

27. What does the pastor pray when he takes their hands in his?

28. Why is the bridal kiss so intense?

Chapter 11 Questions

1. Why is Thumbnail to be even more aware of the messages God sends him for Eli?

2. What does Eli tell Jill after he carries her across the threshold of their home after their honeymoon?

3. When Eli and Jill sit down for coffee, what happens then?

4. How does Eli pitch the first day back after his wedding and honeymoon?

5. What does the MRI and other tests show is causing the pain in Eli's arm?

6. Eli decides to do what about pitching?

7. When Eli and Jill end up in the ghetto, what happens?

8. What does Eli call the most powerful weapon in the world?

9. What does the Bible do?

10. The gang leader asks Eli to do what?

11. What does Eli say and do then?

12. How does Eli treat the gang members when they come to the game?

13. What do Eli and Sam's churches tell them about outreach to the gang members?

14. Next, what do Sam and Eli decide to do?

15. When Eli's mind goes back to the gang around his car, what does he want for them?

16. What idea hits Eli as he is listening to Christian music with Jill singing to the music?

17. Eli is offered what to control the pain in his arm?

18. How does Eli help Jamaal's buddy who is really into drugs?

19. Does Eli's team make it into the World Series?

20. Who is Stuart?

21. When will they start the church?

Chapter 12 Questions

1. How is Eli's shoulder feeling in Game One of the World Series?

2. What did Eli and Sam see when they drove through the ghettos?
3. Does Eli start in the final game of the World Series?
4. When does Eli come in to pitch?
5. Describe Todd Rucket, the batter that Eli is facing.
6. What went through Eli's mind when he faced Todd? What did Eli pray?
7. What was the first pitch Eli threw? What happened?
8. What was the second pitch Eli threw? What happened?
9. Rucket does what to break Eli's concentration?
10. The look Eli gives Rucket says what?
11. Rucket's look to Eli says what?
12. What happened with the third pitch?
13. What did Rucket do next?
14. What happened with the last two batters?
15. Did Los Angeles win the World Series?
16. Eli says this is the reason for his success. What is it?

Teachers and home-school parents, you can get the answers at no additional cost by sending a request to michaelgoldsmith997@yahoo.com.